Ruby leaned her head against Hamilton's chest and closed her eyes.

For one brief moment in her life she felt completely at peace, completely content. His arms were strong and secure, making her feel protected and cherished. She'd been searching for most of her life for such a moment as this, and even though she'd told herself to give Hamilton a wide berth she was not only going to accept this moment but enjoy it as well. If only the world could stay like this for ever…

'Well done,' he murmured near her ear.

'You too,' she replied, lifting her head to look up at him. She realised it was a mistake the second she'd done it. Being in his arms, staring up into his eyes, feeling the overwhelming sensations of deep attraction flooding her entire being… She swallowed, unable to move.

Hamilton looked down into her beautiful face, his gaze flicking to take in her luscious lips. It would take nothing to lower his head the remaining distance, to give them both what they seemed to want. Ruby was in his arms, looking at him as though she wanted nothing more than for him to do exactly that…

Dear Reader

It was great to be able to tell Hamilton's story, especially as he'd been waiting so patiently. We feel as though we've known him since he was a nine-year-old boy, learning as his big brothers surrounded him, breaking the terrible news of the death of his parents—Cameron and Hannah. By the age of seventeen, though, Hamilton was a typical teenage boy who loved playing sport more than doing his homework, but thankfully he found the path that was right for him and headed to medical school. Now a thirty-year-old man, he's ready for fun and adventure—but he's certainly not at all ready to lose his heart to Miss Ruby Valentine!

We knew, when creating the woman who was perfect for Hamilton, that she'd have to be someone special—someone who not only needed what he could give but also would be able to give him something super-special in return. And that's exactly what Ruby does. Poor Ruby has also had her fair share of tragedy, and it's this loss which ultimately helps her to bond with Hamilton. Not only is he able to tease her, to make her laugh, but when he looks at her with those deep blue eyes Ruby's heart can't help but respond.

We hope you enjoy getting to know Ruby and Hamilton, as well as revisiting the world of those gorgeous Goldmark men.

Warmest regards

Lucy Clark

FALLING FOR DR FEARLESS

BY
LUCY CLARK

First published in Great Britain 2012
by Mills & Boon, an imprint of Harlequin (UK) Limited.
Large Print edition 2013
Harlequin (UK) Limited, Eton House,
18-24 Paradise Road, Richmond, Surrey TW9 1SR

© Anne Clark & Peter Clark 2012

ISBN: 978 0 263 23087 1

Printed and bound in Great Britain
by CPI Antony Rowe, Chippenham, Wiltshire

Lucy Clark is actually a husband-and-wife writing team. They enjoy taking holidays with their children, during which they discuss and develop new ideas for their books using the fantastic Australian scenery. They use their daily walks to talk over characterisation and fine details of the wonderful stories they produce, and are avid movie buffs. They live on the edge of a popular wine district in South Australia with their two children, and enjoy spending family time together at weekends.

Recent titles by the same author:

DIAMOND RING FOR THE ICE QUEEN
THE BOSS SHE CAN'T RESIST
WEDDING ON THE BABY WARD
SPECIAL CARE BABY MIRACLE
DOCTOR DIAMOND IN THE ROUGH
THE DOCTOR'S SOCIETY SWEETHEART
THE DOCTOR'S DOUBLE TROUBLE

**These books are also available in eBook format
from www.millsandboon.co.uk**

CHAPTER ONE

HAMILTON cranked up the music and enjoyed the feel of the warm summer breeze flowing around him, glad he'd taken the top off his car at the last town he'd stopped at. It was a brand-new year and one he was looking forward to, especially after the busyness of the last few.

He'd finally finished medical school, passing with marks not only to rival but to beat his older brothers'. That alone had given him great satisfaction. The youngest of five boys, Hamilton had always had someone telling him what to do. Like most younger siblings, he'd been locked in a game of 'catch-up', wanting to do more than he was capable of, and always wishing he was older.

Now he *was* older and on a more equal footing with his brothers. He'd even finished his two-year GP training in eighteen months, thanks to the volunteer work he'd completed with ACT NOW, a Canberra-based volunteer organisation that provided nocturnal outreach welfare and medical aid to those in need.

Last year he'd started his diploma in emergency medicine and everything had been going fine until… Hamilton shook his head, refusing to think about *her*. Thankfully, he'd been able to finish his training out of the country, working with Pacific Medical Aid on the island nation of Tarparnii, performing emergency medicine under the watchful eye of his friend and colleague Daniel Tarvon.

Hamilton would have stayed in Tarparnii for at least another six months but his cousin Brandon had contacted him, asking for help. Poor Brandon had been crossed in love and as Hamilton's own scars were less than a year old, he was more than willing to help his cousin in any way he could.

Yes, the last few years had been busy but the most important event in Hamilton's life was that he'd finally finished paying off his pride and joy—his Jaguar E-Cabriolet. He laughed again as he drove along, determined to leave his past behind him and look forward to the next big adventure.

* * *

'He's late, Vi.'

'He'll be fine,' Viola replied as she pulled a fresh hot apple pie from the oven. 'Is the unit ready? I hope Brandon didn't leave it in a mess.'

'I've already checked it.' Ruby Valentine sat down at the dining room table with a stack of paperwork. 'I'm still annoyed at Brandon for taking off like he did.' Ruby shook her head. 'Why couldn't he wait around one more day to show Hamilton the ropes?'

'You know what he's like,' Viola replied, listening with only half an ear. 'When he gets an idea in his head, it's impossible to get it out.'

'Tell me about it.'

'You weren't snowed under in the clinic today, were you?' Viola set the pie to cool and pulled out a bag of potatoes. 'Brandon assured me you'd be all right to cope.'

Ruby rolled her eyes and shook her head. 'I always cope, Vi. All my life I've coped and I'll keep on coping.' She was a survivor—literally. Her parents had died but she had survived and for a long time she'd suffered from survivor's guilt. It was only thanks to Viola and her late husband,

Bill, that Ruby was more calm and content than she'd been as a troubled fifteen-year-old.

Viola left the kitchen, wiping her hands on her apron before crossing to Ruby's side, placing a hand lovingly on her head. Ruby sighed and put her pen down. 'Don't be mad at Brandon,' Viola said softly. 'He just needs some space. When a woman's heart is broken, she pulls herself together and soldiers on, but when a man's heart is…how did he put it?'

'Crushed beyond repair,' Ruby provided blandly.

'Yes, well, when that happens, men need a change of scenery. Besides, he'll only be gone for six months *and* he did organise for Hamilton to fill in for him. At least he didn't leave you completely in the lurch as far as the practice went.' Viola kissed Ruby's cheek and returned to the kitchen to make a start on the potatoes.

'We'll just have to see how well Hamilton fits in,' Ruby said. 'And as he was due to arrive an hour ago, he's not off to a very good start. Lewisville is a small, intimate town and people don't take too kindly to outsiders, especially when it's a city doctor coming here to tell them what's what.'

'Yes, but Hamilton isn't just *any* doctor. He's

a Goldmark.' Viola chuckled. 'Fits in perfectly at the Goldmark Family Medical Practice, don't you think?'

Ruby wasn't at all sure what she thought. The last time she'd seen Hamilton had been at her surrogate father's funeral. Not exactly the most wonderful of occasions. He'd been polite. She'd given him the cold shoulder and hopefully he'd put her attitude down to the fact that she had been grieving.

But it had been the time before that—the first time they'd met, when she'd been an impression-able teenage girl—when he'd crushed her heart beyond repair, or so she'd thought back then. She'd been so besotted with him when he'd come to stay for a few weeks in the January school holi-days. Then she'd embarrassed herself further by trying to kiss him.

Ruby put down the paper she'd read three times over, not seeing a word. She closed her eyes, clearly able to recall the mortified look on Hamilton's face. What had she been thinking?

'You were only fifteen,' she whispered. 'Young, confused and very lonely.' And he'd been so nice to her. 'He probably doesn't even remember.'

'Hmm? Did you say something, love?' Viola asked.

'N—' Ruby stopped and cleared her throat, amazed to find her tone rich and husky. It was all Hamilton's fault. Even thinking about him caused her body to flip into sizzle mode. 'No,' she replied, her voice nice and strong. And that's the way she wanted Hamilton to see her now. Nice and strong. No longer an innocent, mixed-up teen. She was a confident, happy twenty-eight-year-old woman with a steady boyfriend, a great job and a community who thought she was special. Yes, her life was very different now from what it had been thirteen years ago.

Five minutes later, there was the sound of a car stopping near their door and Ruby still hadn't managed to concentrate on a single word of the paperwork spread before her.

'There. That's him now,' Viola announced, wiping her hands on a tea towel and making her way to the front door, a quickness in her step.

'Oh, no?' Ruby retorted with a hint of teasing sarcasm. 'You weren't worried about him at all.'

'Of course I was worried about him. He's family.'

'He's your third cousin, Vi.'

'Second cousin,' Viola corrected. 'Come on. Let's go give him a grand Lewisville welcome.'

Sighing, Ruby stood and walked over to join Viola on the front veranda that ringed the old family home situated on the main street of Lewisville. The town was large enough to house one swimming pool, one tennis court, one primary school and two police officers. The medical practice she ran with her surrogate brother had been inherited from Bill Goldmark, who had passed away seven years ago, just after Ruby's twenty-first birthday. The practice was situated two doors down from the family home but a few years ago Brandon had decided to build a small unit just behind the clinic rooms, which was where he now lived—and where Hamilton would live for the next six months.

'It's not Hamilton!' Viola remarked, concern still beneath her words.

'It's Geoffrey.' Ruby's eyebrows hit her hairline. 'I hope there isn't an emergency.'

'Prefer this to be a social call?' Viola teased softly, as Sergeant Geoffrey Chancellor climbed from his four-wheel-drive vehicle, slipping his police Akubra onto his head to protect him from the mid-afternoon sun.

'Shh. We've only been dating for a few weeks.' Ruby hissed.

'I'm sure Geoffrey would have been delighted to start dating you a few years ago if you'd given him half the chance.' Viola giggled but turned her attention to the police officer walking towards them. 'Hello, dear. Fancy a drink?' she asked.

Ruby looked at him for a moment, then shook her head as she noted the stiffness of his posture and the firm set of his mouth. 'Something's wrong?'

'Actually, yes.' His smile was short as he nodded politely towards Viola, showing her respect. 'Ian's just received a report of an accident not too far out of town. I was just coming back from the Whites' place when the call came so I thought I'd stop in here. As we both have to go, it would be easier if we went together.'

'Good thinking,' Ruby said, and headed back inside, moving quickly. 'I'll just grab my emergency bag. Do you have any other details?'

'It's not Hamilton, is it?' Viola asked, wringing her hands with concern.

'He's your nephew, right?' Geoffrey confirmed.

Viola shook her head. 'Cousin—well, cousin by marriage. Well, technically, he's—'

'Not now, Vi.' Ruby directed her comments to Geoffrey. 'Any other news?' she asked, putting on her bush hat and slipping her sunglasses into place. She'd already checked her bag and was walking back out to the veranda.

'Report was that a car had hit a roo. Two people involved.'

'No idea who called it in?'

'Ian said it was a man but he didn't give his name.'

'Right.' Ruby kissed her surrogate mother on the cheek and headed for the police car. Geoffrey raised his hat politely towards Viola, then swatted away a few flies in the typical Australian salute before walking around to the passenger side of the car, but he was too late to open the door for Ruby as she was already climbing quickly inside.

'What about Joan?' Ruby asked as Geoffrey slid behind the wheel. 'Will she meet us there with the ambulance?'

'That's the plan. Ready?'

'You two be careful,' Viola called as Geoffrey

started the engine. 'And call me when you know news. Even if it's bad news,' she continued.

Ruby nodded. 'I'm sure it's not Hamilton, Vi. He probably stopped too long in Wagga Wagga or was held up in Canberra, leaving later than anticipated. Everything will be fine.'

'So…Hamilton's coming back, eh?' Geoffrey nodded slowly as he pulled out onto the road. 'Do you remember him coming to town all those years ago?'

Ruby closed her eyes, not wanting to even *think* about it, let alone *talk* about it. Her silence didn't seem to bother Geoffrey as he continued to reminisce.

'Two weeks he was here. That January was a real scorcher, eh? Remember, Ruby?' He reached over and touched her hand. Ruby opened her eyes and looked at him, nodding in answer to his question.

'Didn't stop the bush dance from going ahead. Of course it was nowhere near the grand affair it is now but out here a dance is a dance and everyone came. I'd been looking forward to it because it was my last bush dance for a while.'

'Where…where did you go?' she asked, trying to remember Geoffrey back then, but as he'd been twenty years old, he'd been well and truly out of her notice.

'I went to the police academy. Remember?'

'Yes, I remember now,' she replied, wishing he would change the subject.

'Hamilton was about to start his last year of high school and you were still trying to find your feet after your tragedy eight months prior to that.' Geoffrey talked without malice about her 'tragedy', and given that he'd been through quite a few of his own tragedies, ending up at sixteen coming to live at the teen shelter and refuge Viola ran here in Lewisville, she knew he understood her emotions rather well. Geoffrey's choice had been to come and live in the middle of nowhere and make good—or go to a juvenile detention facility. He had always been grateful to Viola and Bill for knocking some sense into him and giving him a second chance.

'You danced quite a bit with Hamilton that night, if I recall correctly.'

Ruby tried not to blush and turned her face away, looking out the window at the passing scenery, pictures of distant memories starting to float before her eyes, refusing to stay silent. She'd been almost sixteen, had never been kissed, and she'd so desperately wanted Hamilton to kiss her that night. Had Geoffrey been able to see that, too? Had the whole town realised she'd had the biggest crush ever on Brandon's distant cousin? 'I danced a lot with quite a few people,' she rationalised, and Geoffrey agreed.

'We all did. Those dances are fun. Can't wait for the one coming up, even though I'll be on duty. How about you, Ruby? Eager to dance the night away?' He patted her hand once more, not seeming aware of her discomfort. 'I'll bet Hamilton will be more than delighted to whisk you around the dance floor, for old times' sake.' He chuckled. 'Just as well I'm not the jealous type, hey.'

She thought about Hamilton dancing with her again, holding her close, her small hand in his large one, their knees knocking as they stepped in the wrong direction, the way they would secretly smile and laugh and gaze into each other's eyes.

Ruby swallowed, annoyed when her pulse rate started to increase at the mere thought of dancing once more with the man who'd broken her young heart. No. She wasn't looking forward to working with him or dancing with him. In fact, she wasn't looking forward to any of it at all.

Hamilton looked up at the main road. Straight. Flat. Not a car for miles, except for the crumpled one he was now trying to find a way into. Two people had been trapped in the car when he'd come across the accident. He'd instantly slowed down, parking the Jaguar a safe distance away before grabbing his emergency medical bag from the passenger seat and heading back to inspect the wreckage. He was glad his cellphone had been able to get reception so he could report the emergency and request attendance.

The sedan had hit a kangaroo, even though the fresh skid marks on the road showed the driver had tried to swerve. The car had rolled once before coming to rest against a boulder not too far from the edge of the road. Hamilton had managed to prise open the passenger door. The woman had been dazed and confused but only with minor bruises and injuries. She'd had blood on her head where she'd hit it against the dashboard but after a quick inspection, asking her name and checking she could move her arms and legs, he'd concluded her wounds were only superficial. He'd laid her down away from the car, the slight smell of petrol mixing with the heat.

The second person wasn't so easily accessible, the driver's side of the vehicle being more bent and out of shape than the passenger side. As he'd walked around the car, he'd realised that the fuel tank had definitely been ruptured and that it would be best to remove the remaining occupant as soon as possible.

Sitting carefully in the passenger side, he was able to feel the unconscious man's neck for a carotid pulse and while it wasn't as strong as he would have liked, it was definitely there. 'Can you hear me?' he called, but received no response. He manoeuvred around so he could check the man's pupils and was pleased to find them reacting to light. Next, he felt for a pulse and checked the airways were clear. 'Hang in there, mate. Just gotta check your legs, make sure you're not trapped before I get you out of this mess.'

Thankfully, in his emergency medical kit he'd packed a cervical collar and fitted it around the man's neck. Next, he looked at the man's legs; pleased to see they were all right but would require some careful manoeuvring if he was going to be able to get him out via the rear passenger door.

With his reconnaissance completed, Hamilton untangled the phone charger from the man's left ankle. 'Come on,' he said to the man. 'There's no way I can get you out through your side of the car, mate. We're gonna have to go cross-country out the rear passenger side because that fuel stench is getting worse and in this heat I'm not taking any chances.' He checked the man's pulse and airways again and found it the same as before. 'Right. What I'm going to do is lie the seat as far back as I can get it. Then I'll slide you out the rear passenger door. OK?' As he talked, he was relieved when the man murmured something incoherent in response. 'Yes! You're still with me. Excellent.' Hamilton was elated. 'Now, let's get you out of here.' Hamilton started to angle himself so he'd be in the right position. It was squishy and uncomfortable and slow going but he was determined to get them both out of the car before the fuel ignited and exploded.

'It's not gonna be easy,' he continued, talking to the man, who kept murmuring as Hamilton continued to contort himself around, making sure he was in the right position before he moved the patient. 'But just as well for you that I grew up with four older brothers and as such have been used to tug-o'-wars. I know how to heave with the best of 'em. You'll be right.'

Hamilton breathed in, wrinkling his nose at the surrounding fuel smell. 'Yep. Getting worse, or is that just my senses heightening because we're in a dangerous situation?' he asked. 'I know this isn't ideal…' He unwrapped a surgical scalpel he'd retrieved from his medical kit, ready to cut the seat belt and then support his patient. 'And I apologise for the discomfort you're going to have but there really isn't any other opt—' He broke off. 'Shh.' He paused. 'Hear that?'

Hamilton lifted his head, shifting slightly as he peered out at what was left of the front of the car. 'Is that what I think it is?' Hope surged through him as he saw a police car heading down the flat, straight road towards him. He put the scalpel back into the packet, breathing a sigh of relief that reinforcements had arrived. The police car, with lights flashing but no sirens on, slowed down and stopped not too far from the crashed car. The occupants climbed out and rushed over. Hamilton grinned and held up a hand in greeting as a woman looked into the cabin.

'Hamilton!'

The only people who knew him out here were family. It couldn't be Viola. Rescuing teenagers, listening to their woes, providing food and shelter for those in need—that was Viola's calling, not attending accident sites. No, it had to be…

'Ruby?'

'Who else would I be?' she snapped.

Hamilton shifted. 'Excellent. Glad you're here. I've managed to get one patient free but as you can see, the other one is neatly trapped. We can get him out through the rear passenger door but if you've got some sort of Patslide in the back of your vehicle, it would greatly assist.'

The cop who was inspecting the car, looked inside. 'I can arrange to have the jaws of life brought to us,' the man said, and it was only belatedly that Hamilton recognised the voice.

'Geoffrey? Blimey. It's a reunion.' Hamilton's words were filled with surprise but he was still concentrating on the job at hand. 'The jaws of life would be great but only if you also have a fire extinguisher. The fuel line's ruptured and the leaking is getting worse.'

'I'll get the Patslide,' Ruby stated as she headed around to the rear of the police vehicle. 'Geoffrey, if you could take care of the whole "car not exploding" thing, that would be great.' Her voice was brisk and brooked no argument, but Hamilton couldn't help raise an eyebrow at her dictatorial tone. Little Ruby? Cute little Ruby had obviously grown up and was now quite confident in what she was doing. It was great.

He checked his patient again, telling him the change in plans as he watched Ruby carry the Patslide towards the vehicle. 'At least Vi will be glad it wasn't *you* in the accident,' she remarked drolly as she opened the back passenger door.

'Why would she think it was me?' he asked.

'Because you were expected an hour ago?'

'I was?'

'Sure. Brandon told us you'd be here—'

'I never gave him a time,' Hamilton interjected, feeling a little annoyed. He'd been enjoying his drive and had decided to specifically not give a time as he'd wanted to stop along the way if something took his fancy. This was his next big adventure and he wanted to soak it up—every second of it. Apart from Bill's funeral when he'd stopped in Lewisville overnight, the only other time he'd spent in the Outback had been the two-week vacation he'd had here one January, years and years ago. Although he'd had a magnificent time, living and working in the Outback for an extended period was something he'd never done before, hence why he'd been only too happy to help when Brandon had asked.

'I'm sorry if your mother's been worrying but I never said I'd be arriving at any given time. I understood my duties in Lewisville didn't start until tomorrow.'

'They don't.' She turned away from him and called to Geoffrey to come help them. 'Let's get him out,' she ordered. 'You take point.'

'I'd intended to,' he remarked, and again she found herself cutting into her tongue with her teeth as she held back the comments that came instantly to mind, none of them complimentary. 'You support his neck and Geoffrey and I will get the Patslide into position and then I'll need you to—'

'I know what needs to be done, Hamilton. I can see for myself how it's going to work.'

'I thought you said *I* was taking point. I'm just trying to make sure we're both on the same page. How am I supposed to know if you're up to date with rescuing procedures and protocols?'

'Let's just get this done,' she snapped, knowing it would be futile to argue with him at this point. Hamilton went through the routine of checking his patient's vital signs, pleased when the man responded with more than a brief murmur. After giving him something for the pain, they were ready to move him. By the time they'd accomplished their objective, an ambulance had pulled up close by.

'Lewisville has an ambulance?' Hamilton asked, impressed.

'Obviously,' Ruby replied dryly.

'The little town's growing up.' He chuckled and Ruby tried not to grind her teeth at the hint of degradation she could hear in his tone. They shifted their patient to the ambulance stretcher and settled him in the back of the vehicle, giving him oxygen before Ruby reached for the equipment to set up an IV drip. She had to keep busy, had to do her best to ignore the high-handedness of the man who was, in essence, going to be her partner for the next six months.

He was holding out his hand, introducing himself to Joan, Lewisville's paramedic-cum-receptionist. Hamilton was smiling. Joan was reciprocating, even fluttering her eyelashes a little in his direction. What had come over the level-headed woman? Sure, Ruby could admit that Hamilton was handsome—all the Goldmark men were—but they were at an accident site, treating patients, not at a nightclub, flirting. It wasn't Joan's fault she was smitten. It was Hamilton's fault for turning on the charm at such an inappropriate moment.

'Joan?' Ruby's voice was a little sharper than she'd intended, and Joan instantly jerked her hand out of Hamilton's. When the paramedic turned to look at her, there was a tell-tale blush of embarrassment in her cheeks. 'Would you minding checking on the other patient, please?' Ruby pointed in the direction of where Hamilton had left the female passenger waiting on the roadside. Joan instantly nodded and after grabbing an emergency kit headed over to the woman.

Hamilton walked towards her, climbing into the ambulance and reaching around Ruby for a pair of gloves. Ruby tried not to flinch as his arm brushed across her back, causing a deep and suddenly familiar warmth to spread down her spine.

'I can take care of this patient. You go and help…Joan, is it?'

'Oh, you *flirt* with her but instantly forget her name, is that it?'

'I wasn't flirting. I was introducing myself.'

Ruby shook her head, annoyed she'd let her emotions get the better of her. 'Joan is more than capable—' Ruby began, trying not to be affected by the close proximity of his body. Even though it was now after four o'clock and he'd probably been driving for most of the day, she couldn't believe the subtle spicy scent of his cologne as it teased at her senses.

'I've no doubt about it but I've probably had more experience than you with accidents such as this, especially over in Tarparnii where they rarely wear seat belts at all. At least this fellow had the brains to buckle up or there's no telling where his brains might have ended up.'

'Charming,' Ruby said, and shifted from the ambulance, doing her best to ensure they didn't touch again. She needed to get out of there before she socked the overbearing Hamilton with her fist—right in the kisser. She stalked over to where Joan was chatting to the injured woman, cleaning up cuts and bruises and applying first aid. 'Everything fine?' she asked.

'Everything's fine and under control,' Joan remarked, then stood and spoke softly to Ruby so the patient couldn't hear. 'She'll have to go back to town in Geoffrey's car as I can't fit both of them in the ambulance.'

Ruby momentarily glanced over to where Geoffrey was coming around to the front of the car, fire extinguisher still in hand. It was then, for the first time since she'd arrived, that she noticed the large red kangaroo, the cause of the accident, lying by the road on the other side. She shook her head. She'd completely forgotten to check it, to see whether it was actually dead. If it wasn't, then one of them would need to put it out of its misery. As she was the one currently without a job to do, she took control and headed across, walking more carefully and tentatively as she came closer to the large, supine animal.

She'd known of cases where the animal had been stunned, knocked unconscious by the impact, and a while later had scrambled to its feet, jumping away groggily. Looking at the animal now, she could see that that wasn't the case. This one had been badly injured. Too badly for them to do anything about it. Cars hit kangaroos. It was a fact of Outback life and one she'd accepted at an early age.

Walking to the rear of Geoffrey's police car, she extracted one cartridge of ammunition from the safety box and placed it into the rifle. Snapping the weapon back together, Ruby walked with a heavy heart. She hated doing this to the animal but she hated seeing it suffer even more. Putting it out of its misery was the humane thing to do.

'Ruby!' Hamilton was gobsmacked when he saw her walking with the gun. 'Ruby? Ruby? What are you doing?' he called urgently, stepping from the ambulance for a moment, his calls causing Geoffrey to stop what he was doing.

'I thought it was dead,' Geoffrey said, a hint of

apology in his tone. Ruby only shook her head before taking aim and doing what needed to be done.

Hamilton stood by the ambulance, watching the scene unfold before him. He knew this sort of thing happened in the Outback. He knew it was the way of life. He knew what she was doing wasn't wrong, that putting the roo out of its pain was the humane thing to do, but it was the fact that it was little Ruby Valentine doing it. She was walking around, toting a large rifle in her hands *and* using it with expert precision.

He jumped as the shot rang out but it was then he noted one very important fact.

Little Ruby Valentine wasn't a mixed-up teenager any more. She wasn't a medical student either. She was a fully grown woman, a qualified general practitioner who obviously knew the ways of the Outback far better than he did. For the first time in years Hamilton stopped and really looked at her.

Her long brown hair was pulled into a no-nonsense ponytail, low on her neck so it didn't knock her bush hat from her head. She was dressed in a pair of denim jeans, runners and a ruby-red cotton shirt. She turned to face him, the rifle in her hands as she ejected the empty cartridge. He saw the pain and anguish in her green eyes as she stared at him but he also noted the determined jut of her chin.

'Wow,' he whispered, unable to completely comprehend her beauty. 'Definitely grown up.'

CHAPTER TWO

HALF an hour later, they were all on their way back to Lewisville, where the helicopter would meet them to transfer both patients to Broken Hill Base Hospital. His name was Christos. He and his wife, Marcia, had been enjoying themselves travelling around in the Australian Outback, and while they'd been warned about the dangers of kangaroos on the road, they hadn't realised just how quickly a roo could jump out of nowhere.

When Hamilton was satisfied with Marcia's condition, Geoffrey drove her back to Lewisville in his police four-wheel-drive. Ruby went with Christos in the ambulance and Hamilton jumped back into his sports car and headed after them, bringing up the rear of the convoy. The main street of Lewisville hadn't changed all that much from what Hamilton could remember. There were several houses, a petrol station, a general store and the medical clinic. There was also one very important building, the staple of any and all Outback towns, the backbone of the community—the local pub. As the day was now coming to an end, the main street seemed to be crowded with people heading to their 'local' for an ice-cold beer.

However, it wasn't the pub that held his interest, even though a nice cool drink was definitely in order, but rather the new helipad, situated near the sports oval a few kilometres from Main Street. There was a small building next to the helipad with a garage alongside. Joan parked the ambulance in the garage and he pulled up beside it. Ruby and Joan were able to wheel the ambulance stretcher into the building while he and Geoffrey helped Marcia inside.

The air-conditioning was a relief and apart from a few chairs and a bench with tea- and coffee-making facilities, there was an area set aside for monitoring and checking patients before transferring them to the helicopter's specialised stretchers. After he and Ruby were satisfied with their patients' vital signs, they transferred them to the helicopter.

'You're going to do just fine,' he heard Ruby

telling Christos. 'The staff at Broken Hill Base Hospital will look after both of you.'

'You're not coming?' Marcia's tone was filled with concern as she looked from Ruby to Hamilton and back again.

'Joan will go with you to complete the transfer. She's an excellent paramedic.' Ruby smiled warmly and placed a hand gently onto the woman's shoulders. 'You'll both be fine. I'll ring the hospital tomorrow to check.'

'Thank you.' Marcia reached out a hand to Hamilton. 'You are both angels. You saved our lives.'

'It's all part of the service,' Hamilton replied with a bright smile.

They left their patients and stood back as the chopper was set in motion, its large overhead blades spinning wildly until you could hardly see them they were turning so fast.

'It all turned out well in the end,' he stated. 'Their injuries aren't life-threatening, although Christos will have quite a number of months where he'll need to take things easy.' Hamilton nodded. 'Not a bad beginning for my time in Lewisville.'

'Except for the roo,' Ruby pointed out matter-of-factly, before turning and walking away from the helipad. She closed up the small building then headed out to where Geoffrey's four-wheel-drive was parked on the other side of the ambulance. She looked at the three vehicles and shook her head, noting just how much Hamilton's flashy sports car looked completely out of place in the Outback setting.

'Right,' Geoffrey said, his tone brisk and efficient. 'I need to get back to the accident site. Get that debris cleaned off the road and warn any possible oncoming traffic.' He walked with firm conviction back towards his vehicle. 'I've already organised for Parker to bring his tow truck and meet me there.' With a brief nod in their direction, the police officer climbed inside and wound down the window. Just before he started the engine, he paused and turned to look at them once more. 'Er…welcome back to Lewisville, Ham,' he said. Then his gaze rested on Ruby for a long moment and Hamilton couldn't help but raise an eyebrow at the sweet lingering look he intercepted. 'I'll talk to you later, Ruby.'

'OK.' Ruby nodded and when Hamilton looked

her way, he could see she was a little uncomfortable. As Geoffrey started the engine and drove off with a brief wave, Hamilton leaned against his car.

'So…you and the cop, eh?' There was a teasing tone to his voice.

Ruby rolled her eyes. 'Ugh. You sound just like Brandon.'

He shrugged then spread his arms wide. 'Brothers like to tease. It's a fact of life.' He looked around them, then pointed to the oval. 'I remember this oval very well.'

'You should do. That summer you spent here, you and Brandon practically lived at this oval, playing football every day.'

Hamilton's smile was a nostalgic one. 'I was going to be a professional footballer.'

Right now, she really wished he had remained a footballer because then he wouldn't have become a doctor and he wouldn't have come here to fill in for Brandon and she wouldn't have had to deal with the memories of how she'd thrown herself at him. She closed her eyes for a fraction of a second, willing herself to concentrate. 'I see you changed your mind.'

'Show me a seventeen-year-old kid who's followed through on his first real dream. They're few and far between, Ruby.'

Even the way he said her name was the same as it had been back then, although she was sure his tone was slightly deeper. He'd always held his emphasis on the *u*, as though implying there was something unique and incredibly special about her. At fifteen, she'd fallen for his charm and charisma, hook, line and sinker, only to find he hadn't wanted her at all.

'Can I offer you a lift to your house?' His words cut through her thoughts and the idea of being in such close quarters with him made her body start to tingle. She ignored it.

'It's not far. I can walk.'

'But I might get lost without your expert navigational skills.'

Ruby shook her head and pointed towards the town. 'You go that way, then you turn at the first intersection. Ta-dah! You're there.' She turned and started to walk away but he reached for her arm, stopping her.

'Hey. What have I done wrong?' He immediately released his hold when she glanced down at where he was touching her arm. 'Look, I'm sorry about teasing you for dating the cop. Good for you, so long as you're happy.' He knew he meant the words, was positive he meant the words, and yet even saying them and not having her deny that she was indeed dating Geoffrey gave him a moment's pause. Why? *This was Ruby.* The mixed-up teen who had ended up becoming a part of his extended family. They were friends, right? So why should he care who she dated? Unless the guy was all wrong for her. Then he'd definitely care, and if she was serious about Geoffrey, then as Brandon wasn't around to keep an eye on things, Hamilton silently volunteered for the job.

'Come on. Let me give you a ride.' He smiled at her and Ruby knew she shouldn't be affected yet for some weird reason she was. He had all the trademarks of a Goldmark. Thick dark brown hair, piercing blue eyes, which somehow seemed to be able to see right down into her soul.

Of course, all the Goldmark men were good-looking, but there was something about the deepness of his voice, the honesty in his eyes, the politeness of the gesture as he quickly opened the passenger door for her that differentiated him from the others.

'It's all right. I promise to drive nice and slow.'

Ruby's answer was to huff and shake her head, the bush hat staying firmly in place, her sunglasses in her top pocket. Still, she didn't move and was desperately trying to think up another excuse not to spend any more time with him than she had to. It was going to be a long six months.

'Please, little Ruby?' he tried again, and watched with an increasing sense of doom as Ruby straightened her spine and planted her hands firmly on her hips.

'I am *not* little.'

Hamilton shook his head, deciding silence was his best defence…at least for the moment, until he figured out her moods. Strange, though, as he'd always thought he had quite a good bead on Ruby yet he'd been in her company for less than half a day and she'd already displayed many qualities he'd never known she possessed, especially that she could clearly handle a rifle.

'You always do that,' she continued, anger still bubbling within her. 'You always…smile and look cute when you want something—well, it's not going to work. I'm not an idiotic teenage girl any more, Hamilton Goldmark. You don't need to talk down to me. I'm a trained medical professional and as such ask that you treat me accordingly.' She levelled him with a stare and raised her chin, a hint of defiance in her eyes.

Hamilton blinked in astonished surprise, then at least had the good grace to look contrite. 'I'm sorry, Ruby. I was just teasing. I had no idea that bothered you.' She thought he looked *cute*?

'Of course it does. How do you feel when your brothers talk down to you simply because you're the youngest?'

He shrugged, shifting from one foot to the other, sure she hadn't realised she'd struck a nerve. 'I hate it.'

'And just because I'm two years younger than you, do you think I like it any more than you do?'

'I guess not.' He offered a crooked smile then inclined his head towards the open passenger door. 'And as such, dear colleague of mine, please allow me to drive you back to town. I'd like to see Viola and as it's been quite some time since I was last in Lewisville, I can't actually remember which house is hers.'

'Oh, no!' Ruby gasped, and quickly pulled her phone from her pocket. 'I was supposed to call Vi ages ago.' As she pressed the speed-dial number for her surrogate mother, Hamilton placed his hand on her elbow and steered her towards the car. Thankfully, Ruby didn't protest and sat in the passenger seat, allowing Hamilton to close the door. She pulled on her seat belt, doing her best to ignore the way Hamilton's touch had left warmth shooting up her arm and exploding throughout her entire body.

'Sorry, sorry, sorry,' she said into the phone a moment later. Hamilton slipped into the driver's seat and started the deep, throaty engine. 'We're both fine.' She raised her voice a little over the engine noise. 'Hamilton is here with me and we'll be at your place in about sixty seconds. I'll tell you all about it then.'

'Just so long as you and Hamilton are fine,' Viola returned, before Ruby disconnected the call.

'She worries?' Hamilton asked, and Ruby nodded.

'Far too much.' Ruby slipped on her sunglasses after she put the phone away.

'It's nice, though. Nice to have someone worrying about you.'

Ruby nodded and looked at Hamilton. She'd forgotten how he'd been raised without a mother and father, his parents dying in a freak avalanche when he'd been only nine years old. Hamilton's older brother Edward had been twenty-four when the tragedy had happened, the five Goldmark brothers being left orphans. Thankfully, for Hamilton's sake, his older brother had given up his dream of becoming a surgeon to ensure the rest of the boys could be raised in a stable family environment. That type of environment had instilled in him a strong sense of family, and Ruby was on the fringe of that big, crazy family.

'Do you remember much about your parents?' she asked softly as he drove from the helipad area.

'Small bits and pieces. Fragments of memories which sometimes I'm not sure whether they're real or whether they've been pieced together through a combination of photographs and stories my brothers have told.' He paused for a moment, a frown furrowing his brow as he tried to express himself. 'I guess I *feel* them more than anything else.' He shook his head, his frown clearing. 'I suppose that doesn't make much sense.'

Ruby nodded. 'It makes perfect sense.'

'Of course you, of all people, would understand. Sorry. I just forgot for a moment.'

She shrugged. 'It's no big deal. Turn here.' She pointed to the road that led to the heart of Lewisville—Main Street.

There was no traffic on the road, although the number of vehicles at the pub had almost doubled since they'd driven past on their way to the helipad. 'I guess I'm so used to thinking of you as Viola's surrogate daughter…' He stopped, allowing his sentence to hang in the air for a moment before asking, 'Do you think about your parents often?'

She shook her head. 'Not that much. I still don't have full recollection of the accident, and the psychologists I was forced to see after it happened told me that might be one part of my life I never get back.' She spoke matter-of-factly, as though she'd worked hard to gain so much control over her emotions. 'Fifth house down. The one with all the wind chimes hanging from the veranda.'

It was clear to him that Ruby didn't want to discuss her parents or the accident that had made her an orphan. Hamilton only knew the sketchiest details, told to him by his older brothers. Ruby's parents had been fortune-seekers, heading off on different adventures, preferring to travel the country, seeking gold and opal and all sorts of treasure. Their daughter had travelled with them, being schooled via correspondence, and then one week after her fifteenth birthday, disaster had struck. They'd all been down a mine shaft, Ruby included, when a stick of blasting dynamite had accidentally exploded. Ruby's parents had been killed instantly and Ruby had been practically buried alive, trapped in the mine for well over six hours before being dug out.

Bill Goldmark, his father's cousin, had been the local doctor and had treated Ruby for various injuries, including concussion. Viola had welcomed Ruby to the teen shelter and from there, as Ruby's parents had both been only children and it appeared she hadn't had any relatives waiting to claim her, Bill and Viola had taken her in, caring for her as if she were their own daughter.

Now, as he parked the car outside an old weatherboard home that looked to have been recently painted, Hamilton started to look at Ruby differently. She may have matured a lot since he'd last seen her but he was beginning to realise there was still so much he *didn't* know about her and from what he'd seen since they'd first met up again, he needed to rectify that while he was here.

'Hamilton!' Viola opened her arms wide and hugged him close. 'Have you grown since I last saw you?'

'I've sort of stopped growing, Viola—about a decade ago,' Hamilton remarked with a smile as he kissed her cheek. 'You, however, look more and more lovely every time we meet.'

Viola giggled. 'Oh, get away with you.' She tapped playfully at his arm. 'You've certainly inherited the Goldmark charm. That's how Bill won me over. He proposed three times. Did you know that?'

'I didn't.'

'So persistent. So determined to win me and he did but I put him through the hoops first. Needed to be sure it wasn't the charm talking but his heart.' Viola waved a hand in the direction of the kitchen table. 'Sit down, dear. I've already popped the kettle on, or would you like a coldie?'

'Tea's fine, thanks.' Hamilton glanced around the room. Nothing seemed to have changed since the last time he'd been here, which had been seven years ago when Viola's husband, Bill, had passed away.

There were books and ornaments and knick-knacks around the place, doilies on tables and a lot of framed photographs on bookshelves and on the walls. He looked at the one of Viola and Bill's wedding, smiling at the best man and the bridesmaid—his parents. His gut tightened and for one brief moment his heart pounded with sadness for the parents he'd lost so many years ago.

'It's been quite a scorcher today,' Viola chattered, 'but it's gonna rain soon and that should cool things down, at least for a bit.'

'Rain? How can you tell?' Hamilton raised his eyebrows as he turned from staring at the photograph. Ruby was busy clearing away a pile of papers from the table where she'd obviously been working.

'It's the wet season. We get a lot of rain this time of year. Not every day like they do in the

Northern Territory but at least a couple of times a week and usually all around the same time. Five-thirty to six o'clock.'

'Really?' He walked to the front screen door, looking out. The breeze had started to pick up but it wasn't a cool breeze like he was used to back home in Oodnaminaby and Canberra. It was still rather warm, the humidity in the air starting to rise.

'Go and sit outside if you like,' Viola suggested. 'I'll bring you and Ruby a nice cup of tea and you can watch the rain.' With that, Viola shooed them outside and Ruby once more found herself alone with Hamilton.

'I've never...watched rain before. I've sat and watched it snow but that was probably because Edward wouldn't let me go outside and play.'

Ruby inclined her head towards the front veranda and opened the door. 'It's quite relaxing, actually.'

'You've done it before? Just...sat and watched the rain?'

Ruby's smile was instant and Hamilton couldn't believe how the action really lit up her beautiful features, her green eyes twinkling with merri-

ment. 'Life is different here from the big city.'
Ruby sat down on the veranda swing, feeling
a little self-conscious as she wondered whether
Hamilton was going to come and sit next to her.
She shook the thought away the instant it came.
What did it matter where he sat? They were old
family friends, right? She was dating Geoffrey.
Nothing would happen between them and she
knew that, so why was she worrying about where
he might sit? 'At least the regular rain makes all
the trees and grass green for a while,' she said,
as a way of controlling the nervousness running
through her.

Hamilton came outside and looked up at the
sky, the clouds in the distance starting to roll towards them. 'Arggh,' he gasped, startling her,
and in the next moment he'd raced down the steps
towards his car. 'If it's going to be as wet as you
say, I'd best put the top up on my car!' He began
unbuttoning the hood bag and then tilted the front
seats forward before reaching for the handle and
pulling the roof into place. Ruby watched him,
noticing the way his biceps flexed beneath the
navy blue polo shirt he wore. His long denim-
clad legs strode around the vehicle as he began

securing the soft top, clipping it into place. It may have been over a decade since she'd surreptitiously ogled his body but she couldn't help it and had to admit that he looked even more dangerous now than he had at seventeen. She watched his movements, unable to look away. Did the man have any idea how good he looked? *Get a grip, Ruby.* She closed her eyes for a second, breaking off the thought. Of course he did. He was a man.

A moment later, she heard the unmistakable sound of the first large drop of rain hit the roof above her. Sighing in exasperation, she quickly stood and ran down the steps, coming to the other side of the sports car. 'Hurry up,' she growled as she tugged, her fingers slipping a little on the chrome clip. The rain was increasing, the street around them starting to turn a darker shade of grey as more drops seemed to connect with others.

'Just have to put the windows up,' he murmured, opening one door and winding the window up before leaning through the car, pushing the seats back into position in order to do the other side. Ruby found herself admiring his long frame, especially the way his jeans highlighted his cute butt. As he shifted back, she averted her eyes and quickly turned, heading back to the shelter of the veranda.

Hamilton shut the door, satisfied the top was now secure as the heavens opened up, releasing their harvest. His shirt was drenched within a matter of seconds, the fabric clinging seductively to his torso.

'Hurry up,' Ruby called again, and was astonished to find her voice huskier than usual. She cleared her throat and tried hard to avert her eyes but to no avail, her gaze drinking him in.

'All right, all right.' He laughed as he took the five steps leading up to the veranda with two long strides. 'Whoa!' he said as he ran both hands through his now drenched hair. 'You weren't wrong. This really is one almighty downpour!' He laughed again, the rich sound washing over her like a warm blanket. Ruby was watching him closely, liking the way his hair was slightly sticking up, but a moment later she almost yelped when he pulled his shirt up and over his head, wringing it out.

'Thanks for your help with the roof. I'll have to

remember to keep the top up, although it probably won't matter when it's parked in the garage.'

'Parked in the what?' Ruby forced herself to look away to avoid studying the easily defined contours of his body, to not compare the mental picture she had of him as a handsome seventeen-year-old to the more mature, more experienced, more sexy man before her.

'The garage. Brandon told me he was getting one built.' He raised his voice, having to compete with the noise the rain was making on the corrugated-iron roof.

'He might have planned to do it but with what happened, you know, with Lynn, well, he may not have got around to it. In fact, he didn't.' She continued to look at her hands as she spoke, wishing Vi would hurry up and bring out those drinks she'd promised.

'Then where am I supposed to park my car?' He spread his arms wide, his tone imploring, his wet shirt hanging limply from one hand.

'Like everybody else. Against the kerb on the road.'

'But…it could get wrecked…or stolen.'

Ruby stood, unsure where to look and unsure

she wanted to be so aware of a man she wasn't even sure she liked. 'Then you shouldn't have brought a sports car to the Outback, you great galah.' With that, she turned and headed back inside the house, the screen door shutting firmly behind her.

'You're not having tea?' Viola asked as she carried a small tray with three cups and some freshly baked biscuits towards the door.

'No. Sorry, Vi. I have some urgent things to do.' Ruby continued on to her room, desperate to put as much distance between herself and Hamilton as possible. She'd always known he'd been infuriating. She'd always known he'd rubbed her up the wrong way. How on earth had she expected to work alongside him for six months? She'd only agreed because Brandon had begged her. After his break-up from Lynn, he'd been so desperate to get out of town, to take a break, to do something completely different.

'I'll find you someone to fill in. It's just for six months, Rube,' he'd pleaded. 'Come on, sis. Please?'

Ruby leaned against her bedroom door, the same bedroom she'd had since she'd first come to stay here so many years ago. She'd redecorated, painted, hung different pictures as she'd gone from being a teenager to a serious medical student. This house, this town, the family practice. They'd been her world for so long.

She closed her eyes and an image of Hamilton standing before her, spiky, wet, brown hair, bright blue eyes, smooth, naked torso, came instantly to mind. She tried not to sigh as she recalled every perfect contour. It was clear he was no stranger to working out, his physique well defined. Sighing, she rubbed her itchy fingertips together, wanting to rid herself of the urge to reach out, to see if it felt the same way it had all those years ago.

So Hamilton had a great body. So what? It didn't mean anything. Her life was smooth, comfortable, predictable...perhaps too predictable but now *he'd* come to town, causing her natural equilibrium to shift in rolling waves. Was this a good thing? She wasn't sure. She'd been living in Lewisville for so long, doing what needed to be done and doing it all with a smile on her face, that sometimes she wasn't sure what her life was really about.

Of one thing, though, she was sure. The way

she felt when Geoffrey held her hand, or looked into her eyes, or even pressed a small kiss on her lips was nothing compared to the way Hamilton had made her feel just by standing next to her. Everything had been deeper, intense, powerful, and she'd started to tremble. It was why she'd left, why she'd needed to walk away, to put some distance between them and to try and figure out how on earth Hamilton could still have this unwanted effect.

CHAPTER THREE

RUBY came out of her room, calm and composed, ready to ignore the way her hormones seemed to be overreacting whenever Hamilton smiled at her or looked her way or paid her the slightest bit of extra attention. It was exactly those qualities that had made her fall for him when she'd been a teenager. Surely now, as an adult, she had more self-control!

She shook her head. His charm was lethal and she had to become immune to it—and fast. She still needed to show him around the clinic and she'd be seeing him every day for the next six months but apart from that, she simply had to keep her distance. He was nothing but another colleague who happened to be related to Viola. Thank goodness he'd be sleeping at Brandon's place. Ruby wasn't sure how she would have coped with him sleeping in the next room, sharing a bathroom with her. Pasting on a smile, more for Vi's sake than Hamilton's, she headed back through the house.

'I won't take no for an answer,' she heard Vi saying, and stopped just inside the front door, a thread of dread starting to work its way through her as she listened to their conversation.

'No,' she whispered, but knew full well that Vi would have no doubt invited Hamilton around for dinner. It was what Vi did. She looked after people, caring for them and helping them.

'I wouldn't want to impose.' Hamilton's deep tones filled the air as the rain began to peter out.

'Well, I miss having Brandon around and he used to come for dinner at least four times a week so we'll keep up that tradition, shall we? Or you could come every night, I don't mind. I like cooking and looking after people.'

Hamilton's rich chuckle filled the air. 'Well, in that case...' He rubbed his chin thoughtfully with his thumb and forefinger.

'And after Ruby's shown you around, you can get settled in and then come back for dinner,' Vi continued, quite excited and desperate for him to accept. 'And I've made a fresh apple pie,' she added by way of enticement.

Ruby took a step closer, peering out through the screen door, and watched as Hamilton gave Viola a hug. It seemed not even Vi was able to resist that Goldmark charm.

'You should have led with the pie,' he joked. 'There's no way I can refuse home-made apple pie. Honeysuckle makes amazing sweet pies.'

'Now, she's…Edward's wife, right?' At his confirming nod, Viola laughed. 'I get them all confused but it's so great to see most of Hannah's boys settling down. She would have been so happy to know that house of hers is filled with the noise and love of her grandchildren.' Viola tapped her finger on Hamilton's chest. 'And what about you, eh? Time for you to think about settling down?'

Hamilton chuckled and stepped back to lean against the railing that ringed the veranda. 'I don't think so. Not yet, at any rate. My siblings are doing enough of the multiplying. Darla and Benedict have the most recent addition. Angel, their little girl, is almost eight months old.'

Viola's smile was bright. 'Darla sent me a photograph of Angel. She really does look like a little angel.'

He nodded. 'So, you see, there's absolutely no rush for me. Besides, Bart is still single and he's way older than I am so I'm happy for him to go next.'

'Ahh, I get it,' Viola said. 'You're after a bit of adventure, eh? Finding your own feet, discovering where you fit in the world.'

Hamilton nodded. 'Something like that. Not being tied down, being able to pick and choose where and when I work means I can come here to help out Brandon and gorge myself on delicious apple pie. There's plenty of time—' He turned then and saw Ruby standing at the screen door. He hadn't heard her return but at the first sight of her his heart did a crazy little somersault that momentarily robbed his mind of coherent thought. Good heavens, did the woman have any idea just how incredibly beautiful she was?

'Plenty of time...?' Viola prompted, her back to Ruby. Hamilton quickly returned his gaze to his cousin and forced a smile, astonished that his mouth was suddenly dry.

'Er—plenty of time for marriage.' He cleared his throat. 'There's no rush.' He looked at Ruby. 'Ready to give me a tour of the clinic?'

'Oh, there you are, darling.' Viola turned and smiled. 'Yes, well, off you two go because dinner will be ready soon but only if I finish getting things ready.'

Ruby held the door for Vi, glanced at the tray with two empty tea cups and one clean one and then looked at Hamilton. She tried to ignore the thread of guilt at not staying for a cup of tea, especially after Vi had gone to so much trouble. It had been rude of her to just walk away and she would apologise later, but realising she still felt an attraction for the man who had already broken her young heart had freaked her out—just a little bit. Thankfully now she was back in control of all her faculties.

She would show Hamilton around the clinic, sit across the dinner table from him and work alongside him for the next six months. He was just a locum, filling in for a short period of time. There was no permanence about him. Hadn't he just said as much to Viola? Adventure. The right to choose where and when he worked. She couldn't help but be a little bit envious. Her days were meticulously planned…and that was the way she liked it. Wasn't it? She shook off the confusion.

'Ready?'

'For my clinic tour?'

'Yes.'

'But it's raining.' He jerked his thumb over his shoulder.

'So?'

'We'll get wet.'

'So?' She shrugged her shoulders and walked to the top step. 'You'll dry soon enough. This isn't Snowy Mountains rain, where it drizzles all day and the breeze is cool. Go on, Adventure Man. Live a little.' Her words were teasing as she headed down the steps and started walking down Main Street without waiting for him.

Hamilton blinked one long blink, happily surprised at Ruby's action. She was right and within a few long strides he'd caught up to her, the large drops of rain cooling him down. 'You're spontaneous now?' he checked. 'From what I recall, Brandon and I had trouble cajoling you into doing something crazy with us. You always flatly refused.'

Ruby shook her head. 'Like the time you both wanted me to put my arms in the air and be your goalpost so you could have a competition to see who could kick a football the furthest?'

Hamilton chuckled, the memory returning. 'And you would have made the best-looking goalpost I'd ever kicked a football through.' He shook his head. 'I have no idea why you refused.'

'Or at the January bush dance when you wanted me to spike the punch?'

'Viola was watching us closely,' he protested. 'Neither Brandon nor I could get close to that bowl without her intercepting us. You were our only hope.'

'And you wonder why I refused,' she returned drolly. 'Or the time I refused to help when Luke Cuthbert and Vikie O'Callaghan got married and you wanted me to join you in defacing their car.'

'It wasn't *defacing*,' he corrected. 'It was *decorating*. Confetti, streamers, tin cans tied to the bumper and the words "Just married" written in lipstick on the back window. That was all!'

'Hmm.' She shook her head. 'I doubt you'd appreciate anyone *decorating* your squashed metal beetle you've no doubt spent a fortune on.'

He stopped dead in the street and glared at her, the rain pouring down on him. 'Squashed metal—' He broke off, his jaw hanging open for a moment before he shook his head and tut-tutted, catching up to her. 'I can see I'll need to take you for a drive and *then* we'll see what you really think.' He shook his head. 'Squashed metal beetle indeed,' he grumbled.

Ruby couldn't help but laugh at the dark look on his face. She stopped outside the clinic door, the front veranda of the building providing them with shelter from the rain. As she pulled out her key and opened the locks, Hamilton shook his head and ran his fingers through his wet locks. When she glanced at him, he was once more sporting that spiky-haired look that instantly set her heart racing. With his wet shirt, his long legs, his hypnotic eyes and slight scowl, he looked dark and ominous and scarily sexy. She quickly looked away, her hands fumbling with the lock as she focused her thoughts on opening the door.

'Need some help?' he asked.

'I've got it,' she grumbled, annoyed with herself for allowing him to fluster her. *Distance, Ruby. Keep your distance.* She finally unlocked the door and headed inside, the bell over the door tinkling as she switched on a light so he could see the reception area. 'This is where Joan sits. As she's also a trained paramedic, she'll provide general first aid if necessary. She's also qualified to take blood samples and give immunisations. It just keeps the whole clinic process more smooth if we're not having to do little things like that.'

Ruby moved away from his close proximity, ensuring a safe distance, which was difficult given the Goldmark Family Medical Practice wasn't an enormously large clinic. Hamilton's presence seemed to fill the space and even though he was roughly the same height and build as Brandon, his presence made her feel mildly claustrophobic. She headed up the corridor, keeping her back to him and her tone neutral.

'My clinic room,' she pointed. 'Your clinic room. Kitchenette on the left, Joan's small clinic room on the right and down the back here we have our emergency treatment room.' Ruby took out another set of keys and unlocked the door. 'This is also where our medical and drug supplies are kept, hence the locks.' She opened the door and Hamilton was impressed with the set-up. There was a treatment-cum-operating bed complete with overhead operating lights, rows of cupboards both above and below a bench, a large sink and an up-to-date crash cart. There were other bits of equipment here and there and he nodded, clearly liking what he saw.

He whistled. 'Nice! You're well set up here.' He looked around the room. 'Very impressive.'

'I think you'll find the Lewisville community is adept at raising funds. In fact, next week we're holding a bush dance in order to raise funds for a portable digital imaging machine.'

'Really? The bush dances have become fundraisers as well?' His eyebrows went up at this news and he nodded. 'Good move.' He continued to look around the room. 'Again, very impressive.' He waved an arm at the set-up. 'You could do minor surgical procedures here.'

'Exactly. Emergency only, of course, but as Brandon has his diploma in emergency medicine, he's the one who deals with emergencies.' She glanced his way. 'He told me you've done the same course. Is that right?'

'It is.' Hamilton clenched his jaw. It was the diploma that had caused his life to change, or, more correctly, his first supervisor for the diploma who had wrecked his life. Diana was the last person he wanted to think about right now and he shoved any thoughts of her from his mind. Although this was his first job back in Australia with his new qualifications, he wasn't going to let thoughts of her intrude upon his new adventure.

'Good.' Ruby nodded. 'At least Lewisville and its surrounding communities are well and truly covered for any possible emergency.' They headed back into the corridor, Ruby locking the door after them. 'I have a set of keys for you at home. Sorry. Forgot to pick them up.'

Hamilton shrugged, watching her closely. 'I'll get them at dinner. Besides, it's not as though you live far away.'

Ruby smiled at his words. 'No.'

'What about you, Ruby? Have you done extra study?'

She shook her head. 'I'm not a fan of big cities,' she offered. 'I didn't enjoy Sydney much during medical school. Besides, I'm needed here.'

'But, Ruby, there are other places in the world to do further study than big cities. In fact, in this day and age, with the internet, you can work at a little country hospital and do the coursework online. I did most of my diploma whilst working in Tarparnii.'

'Really? I remember Brandon telling me you you'd started it in Canberra.'

'Yeah. I did.' He shrugged and Ruby couldn't help but notice he seemed a little uncomfortable. 'But that was only for three months. Then I headed off to Tarparnii with PMA and, as that's classified as A and E work, was able to change supervisors and finish it under the guidance of my friend Daniel Tarvon.'

'So…you've come here from Tarparnii?'

'Yes, and I'm scheduled to go back for a further six months when I've finished here.'

Ruby thought on this for a moment. 'You came back because Brandon asked?'

'Yes.'

'Otherwise you would have stayed there for quite some time?'

He nodded slowly, wondering if Brandon had mentioned anything to her about Diana. His immediately family knew about the way the woman had played him for a fool, of course, and then when Brandon had asked Hamilton to fill in for him, his cousin had sounded so incredibly desolate Hamilton had immediately agreed, telling his cousin that he could well understand romantic heartbreak and the urgent need to get away. 'Yes.'

'You came all the way back from Tarparnii to help us out?'

'Sure. That's what family is for, right?' He turned and took a few steps down the corridor towards the front door. Ruby frowned, watching him retreat. His normal joviality had disappeared and her feminine intuition told her he was definitely keeping something back…or running away from something. Why else would he change supervisors in the middle of a degree? It was a new side to Hamilton, one she'd never seen before, and it intrigued her. Perhaps he wasn't the happy-go-lucky, carefree teenager he'd once been.

Before she could ask him any more questions, the bell over the front door rang, which meant someone had come into the clinic. She turned and went to investigate.

'Ned! Hi,' Ruby said to the elderly man who'd come into the clinic.

'Is he here?' Ned asked, excitement in his tone, his eyes bright with delight. A split second later Hamilton appeared behind her and before Ruby could say another word, Ned had crossed to Hamilton's side and was shaking his hand warmly.

'Great to have you here, Dr Goldmark. Fancy that. Another Dr Goldmark coming to Lewisville to replace Dr Goldmark who took over the practice from his father who was, indeed, Dr Goldmark. Astounding. What are the odds?'

'Er...' Hamilton glanced at Ruby, trying to figure out what was going on, but she merely shrugged her shoulders. 'Actually, I have three brothers who—'

Ned wasn't listening as he continued to pump Hamilton's hand. 'Finnegan. Ned Finnegan. Mayor of Hueyton, which encompasses Lewisville and all its districts. Quite a large area for me to cover, especially around election times, but the wife and I live here in town so when I saw you and Ruby coming into the clinic I thought I'd pop by and introduce myself. We're so glad you could fill in for Brandon, especially after what that girl did to him, poor chap, but not to worry, because men recover far easier from a broken heart than a woman. They're always weeping and—'

'Was there something you wanted?' Ruby interjected, keeping her tone sweet but to the point, effectively cutting Ned's drivel short.

'Ah, yes. Of course.' Ned looked over his shoulder at her as though he'd forgotten she was there. Hamilton took the opportunity to remove his hand from Ned's overzealous grip. He guessed the Mayor to be in his late sixties but he appeared to be in excellent health and as strong as an ox, even though he had a rather slim build.

'My darling wife, May, and I would like to invite Dr Goldmark…' he chuckled at the name as though he'd made some hilarious joke '…over for dinner.'

'What a good id—' Ruby began, thinking that would mean she didn't have to sit across the table from him at dinner, trying desperately to stop herself from gazing into his deep blue eyes.

'Sorry.' Hamilton cut her off. 'I promised Viola I'd be around for dinner.'

'But Vi won't mind,' Ruby said.

'Uh-uh.' Hamilton wagged a finger in her direction. 'Family first, and as it's my first night in town, I can think of nothing better than to catch up with my family.' He looked at Ned. 'I'm sure you and your wife understand.'

Ned didn't look as though he understood at all. 'Oh, May will be ever so disappointed. Perhaps she could give Viola a call and talk her into changing your dinner night to—'

Ruby closed her eyes, knowing May Finnegan would indeed be upset at having her invitation turned down. May was the perfect Outback politician's wife and lived to serve others. As much as Ned's high-handedness annoyed Ruby and as much as Hamilton's nearness was causing her body to be in a constant state of flux, she opened her eyes and smiled.

'Why don't you and May come over to our place for dinner?' she said, interrupting Ned in mid-speech. 'Then May can secure a firm invitation from Hamilton in person.'

'Ah—excellent idea. I know May and Viola would love an opportunity to catch up.' He took Hamilton's hand in his yet again and Hamilton took the opportunity to guide the other man to the door.

'Thank you so much for stopping by to welcome me,' he said with bright joviality as he opened the clinic door with his free hand. 'Looking forward to seeing you and your lovely wife at dinner.' Hamilton extracted his hand and with a polite smile closed the door once Ned was on the other side. He turned to face Ruby and pointed an accusing finger in her direction. 'You were going to feed me to the lions. Why?'

Ruby shrugged, trying to not squirm beneath his penetrating gaze. 'I think it's important for you to get to know the community.'

'If you really thought that, you would have taken me to the pub before we came here. There's no better way to meet everyone *en masse* than heading to the local pub.' He advanced slowly towards her and when she took a step back, Ruby found herself coming into contact with the receptionist's desk.

'You have a point. How remiss of me. Shall we go there now?'

He continued to slowly walk towards her. 'I think you're up to something.'

'Me?' she squeaked, and tried to clear her throat. He was drawing closer and she could feel the heat of his body near hers. A thousand different teenage memories zipped through her mind. Hamilton smiling down at her. Hamilton holding her close as they danced together at the bush dance.

Hamilton removing her hands from around his neck, slowly shaking his head, rejecting her advances.

Hamilton chuckled, completely unaware of the turmoil pulsing through her or the way his close proximity was causing utter havoc with her equilibrium. 'Yes, you. I think you're teasing me and do you remember, Miss Ruby, the punishment Brandon invented for every time you teased him?'

'What? You *know* about that?'

'About you teasing Brandon or about the punishment?' He raised one eyebrow but she could see quite clearly in his bright blue eyes that he knew about both.

'No. No. Stop, Hamilton.' She shook her head. 'Don't you *dare* blow a raspberry on my stomach, Hamilton Goldmark!'

His grin was slow, wide and maddening and Ruby instantly put her hands on his chest in what she knew was probably a futile effort to hold him at bay. The moment her hands made contact with his torso, Hamilton felt a powerful heat surge through him and his eyes widened imperceptibly at the touch.

He should have known better than to tease her, not when he'd already been far too aware of how much she'd changed since the last time they'd met. His gaze dipped to look at her mouth and when he saw her perfectly pink lips parted, her chest rising and falling as her breathing increased, the smile slipped from his face. It was only then he was completely conscious of just how close they were. In fact, if he bent his elbows just a smidgen their mouths would be close enough to touch.

'Well…' He swallowed over the huskiness of his tone, looking into her eyes once more, unable to remember anything they'd been talking about and acutely aware of just how much he wanted her. With one swift move he jerked back from the desk and turned to open the front door. 'Actually, I'll give you a reprieve this time,' he said, his back to her. 'I might follow my own advice and go and introduce myself at the pub.' He glanced once in her direction. She was still standing in exactly the same spot, hands by her side, and if he wasn't mistaken, she was also trembling slightly. He closed his eyes, ashamed of his behaviour. She was like family, for goodness' sake.

It was all well and good to realise she'd grown up, changed, matured into an incredibly attractive young woman but quite another thing to almost kiss her.

'I'll see you at dinner,' he choked out, then turned and walked away, the little bell above the door tinkling as he left.

CHAPTER FOUR

'How was the pub?' Viola asked him when he arrived for dinner. Ruby was setting the table with knives and forks and he was instantly aware of every move she made. He closed his eyes for a split second and forced himself to concentrate on answering Viola's question.

'Great. I met lots of new people, settled a dispute and broke up a fight.'

'Parker,' Ruby and Viola said in unison.

'Yeah. That's the guy.'

'He's our resident mechanic and tow-truck driver,' Ruby offered, and Hamilton nodded, still carefully avoiding her gaze. 'Always gets into a bit of a scrap.'

Hamilton smiled and nodded and it all became too much for Ruby with visions of him leaning towards her, their mouths so close, the air around them filled with repressed tension. She quickly excused herself, needing some space.

Hamilton watched her go, trying not to enjoy the way her body moved with such grace when she walked.

'Everyone's OK, though, aren't they?' Viola checked, and Hamilton nodded, heading into the kitchen to lend a helping hand.

'You don't mind that there's two extra people coming for dinner?' he asked.

'I'm more than used to cooking for a whole gaggle. It reminds me of the old days when this house was flooded with teenagers,' she told him with a laugh, then sighed. 'Then it all started getting too much for me and the Murphys took it over, moving it to their farm. Still, I often have people drop in and either stay for dinner or just want a bed for the night. It's good. Makes me feel useful again.'

Hamilton kissed her cheek. 'I think you're amazing,' he whispered.

When the Finnegans arrived, Ruby came out of her room and appeared to be her usual happy self. Hamilton was eager to keep his distance from her, making sure he didn't sit near Ruby or directly across from her. If he had, he'd have ended up staring at her all night long. As it was, he found his gaze wandering in her direction more often than not and each time forced himself to look away.

Ned and May Finnegan were more than content to keep the conversation flowing, if not hijacking it altogether, which meant there were no awkward lulls in conversation. Sometimes it was difficult to get a word in edgeways but Viola was clearly an expert at it and after explaining the family connection between Hamilton and herself, she reached over and patted his hand.

'Do you know, out of all your brothers, you're the one that reminds me the most of your father?'

'Really?' Hamilton was astounded at that.

'Yes, of course. You're vibrant and confident while still being very caring. Cameron may have been quick to temper but he was always quick to cool as well. He also had a sense of impulsiveness about him that your mother fell instantly in love with.'

Hamilton looked at Viola in astonishment. 'How do you know all this?'

'Oh, dear boy.' She stroked his cheek. 'I grew up in the same town as your dad.'

'You did? Why don't I know this?'

'Of course I was a few years younger than both the boys but Bill and I were sweethearts from when we were about sixteen, even though we didn't get married until I was twenty-one. I was there the night your dad first laid eyes on your mother.' Viola smiled and sighed. 'Bill and I had not long been engaged and there was a Christmas dance at the local hall. Your mum was staying with friends in the area and they brought her along to the dance. Well, your dad took one look at Hannah and he said to Bill, 'That's the girl I'm going to marry.' Of course, we both thought he was joking. Cameron always was a kidder but by the end of the night he'd danced with her quite a few times, the two of them hitting it off right from the start.'

'But I was told they met at medical school.' Hamilton was clearly perplexed.

'And they did. That night, after the dance ended, Cameron politely kissed your mother on the cheek, then asked her to marry him.'

'What? No. He can't have.'

Viola levelled him with a glare. 'Were you there?' When Hamilton contritely shook his head, she nodded once. 'Now, shush.'

May giggled and her husband smiled. It was the first time they'd been attentive to someone else all night long. Ruby laughed at Vi, eager for the story to continue. It was interesting hearing about Hamilton's parents, even though she'd never met them.

'Sorry,' he replied.

'Anyway, where was I?'

'My father asked my mother to marry him the night they first met,' he supplied, eager to jog her memory.

'Oh, yes. Well, of course Hannah, thinking he was joking, replied, "Sure. Why not?" Then the next day, when Cameron went over to the house where she was staying, he discovered Hannah's parents had driven up earlier that morning and taken her back to Melbourne. He did manage to get an address for her and he wrote to her a few times but the letters were returned unopened. Her parents didn't approve. She was only seventeen after all.' Viola sipped her drink and shook her head.

'Poor Cameron was heartbroken,' Viola continued a moment later. 'But he soldiered on, never forgetting her. He and Bill went off to medical school together and then a few years later I remember the boys returning to Shepparton, which was where we were living at the time, with Cameron declaring he was the happiest man alive. His lovely Hannah, the woman he still carried a torch for, had not only enrolled at the same medical school but had been looking for a tutor—and he'd offered to help!'

Hamilton nodded. 'Yes, now, that's the story I've been told. Dad was a few years ahead in medical school and tutored Mum. *That's* how they fell in love.'

'She was a bridesmaid at my wedding.' Viola pointed to the framed wedding picture up on the wall. 'And although she and Cameron were married a few years after us, they were the ones blessed with the ability to have a whole gaggle of healthy boys. I had three miscarriages in three years. Then the doctors said we'd better wait a while longer before trying again and when I finally became pregnant with Brandon, I had to stay in bed the whole pregnancy. Wasn't allowed to lift a finger. I hated it at the time but if it meant I could have a healthy baby then I was determined to do it. After he was born, the doctors insisted I have a hysterectomy so although I wanted a whole gaggle of children like Hannah, I was pleased to at least have my one little boy. It wasn't until Brandon was about four that we came to live out here in Lewisville, Bill taking up the post as medical doctor to a town that was in desperate need of love and attention.'

'Here, here,' Ned said robustly, but May put her hand on his and shushed him.

Viola put her arms around Ruby, drawing her close. 'And although I had many years of helping out confused and unruly teenagers, this house often bursting at the seams with people, it wasn't until my darling Ruby came into our lives that I finally felt as though our family was complete.'

Ruby smiled and could feel herself blushing beneath Hamilton's interested gaze. Of course Vi had told her so many times how important she was but Ruby had to admit that given the almost indifferent upbringing she'd had until the age of fifteen, her parents having been often far more interested in their adventurous, treasure-hunting ways than her, Ruby loved hearing Vi saying these words. *Our family was complete.*

'I love my two children very much,' Viola finished, and Ruby kissed her surrogate mother on the cheek.

'Just as we love you,' Ruby said, her words filled with meaning.

Hamilton nodded and smiled at the picture they made together. Ruby with her dark hair and green eyes and Viola with her light grey hair pulled up into a bun and bright blue eyes. They were so different and yet they were definitely connected through the bonds of love. It was nice. 'You're certainly a very special lady, Viola, with the way you've always opened your home to anyone who needed help. All those mixed-up and confused teenagers who just needed someone to listen.'

Viola shrugged. 'Houses should be filled with love and support. Speaking of which, you're welcome to come here any time, for a meal or just for a chat. I don't want to step on your toes or cramp your style but know that you are always welcome.'

Hamilton touched her hand. 'Thank you. I do feel welcome.'

'And you still owe us a dinner,' May reminded him.

'And then Marissa Mandocicelli will want you

to come over,' Viola added. 'She'll make you pasta the—

'Old-fashioned way,' May and Viola said in unison, and Hamilton smiled.

'Oh, and the Eddingtons,' May agreed with a nod. 'They'll want you over to their place for a meal.'

'Sounds as though you'll be well fed.' Ruby stood and started clearing up the dishes. Seeing the smile on Hamilton's face, hearing the delight in his tone as he spoke, remembering the way he'd stood and stared at Viola's wedding photograph earlier that day, the look of deep sadness in his eyes—the man was becoming far too consuming of her thoughts. She didn't even want to think about what had happened at the clinic when he'd leaned in close, their breaths mingling, their mouths almost touching.

The dessert dishes in her hands started to shake and she quickly turned and carried them to the kitchen sink. The sooner he was out of her home the better, and clearing the dishes away was a sure enough hint that it was time for him to leave.

'Well, I think I'll call it a night,' he remarked,

smothering a yawn. 'Apparently I have a busy clinic tomorrow so I'd best get some shut-eye.'

Ruby stayed in the kitchen, leaning back against the sink, wanting to keep as much distance between them as she could. She forced a smile and nodded, watching as he stood from the table, unfolding his tall, lithe frame. She knew what his chest felt like, all firm and sculpted, and she clenched her jaw, banishing the memory to the furthest recesses of her mind.

When he picked up some of the dishes, she took a few steps towards the dining table, holding up her hands to stop him. 'Don't worry about clearing up. I can do it.' The words rushed from her mouth and she forced herself to calm down. 'Er… seven-thirty tomorrow morning sound OK?'

Hamilton watched her for a brief moment, his gaze quickly flicking over her, leaving spots of warmth running through her. 'Seven-thirty's fine. Back home I was used to a half-hour commute to work so as it will now take me one whole minute to get there, we'll have loads of extra time for you to cover anything we…er…missed earlier on.'

Ruby's eyes widened imperceptibly. *Missed?*

Did that mean he was planning on picking up on where he'd left off before heading to the pub? With Hamilton leaning close, looking at her mouth as though it was the most perfect mouth in the world? With her feeling as though she was about to pass out from oxygen starvation because his nearness literally took her breath away? She swallowed and nodded, finding she was unable to speak.

'Good.' He shook hands with both Ned and May before walking around to where Viola was standing, waiting for him. He gave her a warm hug. 'Thanks again. For everything. That apple pie was delicious.'

'See you tomorrow, deary.' Viola hugged him back. 'Ruby? Can you walk Hamilton to the door, please? I just need to show May some of my new quilting squares that arrived in the post yesterday.'

'Right, and I'll go use the facilities,' Ned remarked, and within a moment Ruby and Hamilton found themselves alone.

'It's OK,' Hamilton remarked, jerking his thumb towards the door. 'I can see myself out.'

Ruby sighed and stopped him. 'Hamilton.

Wait a moment.' She crossed to a drawer in the kitchen, rummaged around in it for a moment before extracting a set of keys. 'Almost forgot. These are for the unit and the clinic.'

'You just keep them in that drawer, which is accessible to anyone who walks into this house?' he asked, and she could hear the slight hint of censure mixed with disbelief in his tone.

She raised her chin, defiance flashing in her eyes. Hamilton swallowed, drawn in by her vibrant nature. 'If *I* can never find them in that drawer, no one can,' she returned.

'Fair enough.' He weighed the keys in his palm, knowing he should move but wanting to be near her, just for a tad longer.

'Sorry I didn't get to show you the unit.'

'I think I'll manage.' He paused, an awkward silence starting to settle over them. 'Right.' He took a few steps towards the door. 'I guess I'll see you...' When Ruby started following him, he stopped. 'What are you doing?'

Ruby shrugged. 'It's always been Viola's policy to escort guests to the front veranda. Vi calls it good manners and she'd be horrified if I ignored them.'

'But I'm not a guest,' he said as he took a step towards the door. 'I'm family.'

'Manners,' she reiterated, and walked towards him, coming round the far side of the table in order to give him as wide a berth as possible. Shrugging, he turned and headed to the door, Ruby following him out onto the veranda.

'See? Not so difficult after all.' She leaned against the rail, still keeping her distance. Hamilton looked up at the night sky and gasped.

'Wow. The stars really are brighter here.'

'Aren't they bright where you grew up? Oodnaminaby's rural, right? Not a big city?'

'Yes, but here the stars seem to stretch on for ever, and why is it that whenever you say the words "big city" you sound as though you're completely disgusted?'

'Because I am.' She shrugged. 'I just don't like them.'

'Then how on earth did you survive medical school? Weren't you away for extended periods?'

'I was. In Sydney.' She shuddered at the words.

Again there was a hint of disgust in her tone. 'There's a story there. Bad experience? Did some guy hurt you?' Hamilton thumped one fist into his open hand. 'What's his name? I'll take care of him.'

'Easy, pal. I already have one over-protective, chivalrous big brother. I don't need another.' She smiled and tilted her head to the side. 'Are you this protective of your sisters-in-law? Of Lorelai? Of the…women…in your life?'

'Fishing?'

'What?'

He smiled. 'Wanting to find out if I'm attached or single?'

'Oh, you're single. You're Mr *Adventure*, re-member? Not wanting to settle down any time soon.' There was a hint of disgust in her voice. Hamilton paused for a moment, realising she'd obviously overheard his conversation with Viola. He couldn't blame her as they'd hardly been whis-pering. Besides, it was no great secret.

'You say "adventure" as though it's a dirty word. Why?'

Ruby simply shook her head, doing her utmost to ignore his question. If she stayed silent for a moment or two longer, he'd give up and leave. At least, that had been her experience with a lot of men so far, Brandon included. Instead, Hamilton actually moved closer to where she was standing and when he spoke she could hear the gentle probing in his words.

'I don't have far to travel tonight, Ruby, so I've got quite a bit of time to wait. Why is it that you don't like going on adventures? That you don't like big cities? Something's happened.'

'My parents happened. All right?'

The words came out with such force she even surprised herself. Hamilton didn't grin as though he'd won, he didn't frown as though he pitied her. His face remained neutral and it was this neutrality that caused her to expound, now almost desperate for him to understand.

'*They* were adventurers. Other kids always thought it was so cool that I didn't go to school, that I didn't have any rules, that I could just travel with my parents and stop at new places and be free. Well, let me tell you, it wasn't fun. It was terrible always living a nomadic lifestyle and if, because my parents were more interested in the next adventure, the next big treasure rather than spending time with their daughter and ensuring she had a decent education, I prefer to remain in one place, developing a friendship base, then so be it.'

By the time she'd finished, Hamilton's eyebrows had almost hit his hairline. 'Fair enough.' He paused for a moment. 'Although there are many different types of adventures, such as doing an extreme sport, like going abseiling or rock-climbing or—'

'Mining?'

'For some people, yes, but for others adventure might simply be trying something different, changing a routine, stepping outside a comfort zone.'

'Is that what you're doing coming here? Stepping outside your comfort zone?'

'I'm certainly trying something different,' he pointed out. 'Although I came to Lewisville as a teenager, coming for a two-week holiday and working here for six months are two very different things. Hence—adventure.' He spread his arms wide.

'Well…good for you, Hamilton. I hope you enjoy your adventure in Lewisville, and that *does* include being on time for work tomorrow.'

Hamilton chuckled, the rich, deep sound filling the air, surrounding her like a comfortable blanket. 'Yes, boss. I'll see you then. Goodnight, Ruby. Sleep sweet.'

''Night,' she said softly, hugging her arms around her middle. He turned slowly and started walking down the street and Ruby sank down on to the veranda swing, unable to wipe the smile from her face. What was it about Hamilton that made her feel as though she'd been through the full gamut of emotions in less than half a day?

She sat there for a while, standing to say goodnight to the Finnegans when they left and then returning to the seat. Viola came to sit beside her.

'What a lovely night. Hamilton is certainly Mr Charming, isn't he?' She sighed. 'So much like his father. Tall, dark and handsome. Confident and filled with that typical Goldmark charisma they all seem to inherit.' Viola sighed and started to swing the seat. 'My Bill had it in spades. That powerful charisma. The charm. The smile. So dashing. So…breathtaking.'

Ruby took Vi's hand. 'You miss him, don't you?'

Viola smiled, her tone thick as she answered. 'Every day, dear.'

They sat in silence for a while before Ruby sighed. 'Vi, do you think I'll ever meet someone who makes me feel the way you felt about Bill?'

Viola chuckled. 'Oh, I think there's a very high probability, darling.'

Ruby frowned and looked at Vi. 'What's that meant to mean?'

'I think you've already met him, sweetheart, but you just don't realise it yet.'

'Who? Geoffrey?'

Viola didn't answer, just smiled. Ruby sat back and looked back up at the sky. 'Geoffrey's a sweet man. Nice. Dependable.'

'But he doesn't exactly get your heart pumping?'

'Vi!'

Viola giggled. 'Oh, darling. You'll sort it all out. You're one smart cookie.'

Geoffrey would be the ideal husband. He would offer her a constant, steady life here in Lewisville where she could continue on the way she'd always been. Helping, providing medical support, living near her family, being a part of the community. Wasn't that what she wanted?

The thought of staying here in Lewisville all

the rest of her days brought to the surface a spark of rebellion. She wanted to travel, to see what else was out there in the big wide world, but she couldn't leave the town in the lurch. They depended on her, needed her. Even tonight May had pinned her down to a meeting to discuss the next quilting bee and Ned had demanded her time tomorrow afternoon to go over final preparations for the bush dance.

She was on every committee the town had and as a doctor she had a certain amount of standing and influence over certain events. The fact that the district was willing to rally around, to support and give money to raise funds for medical equipment, was something she couldn't overlook. The proceeds from the bush dance would mean the clinic could purchase the latest technology in portable digital imaging. It meant if someone were to break their arm, she and Brandon would be able to X-ray it on the spot and from there decide the necessary treatment. It would mean fewer helicopter rides to and from Broken Hill hospital, it would mean fewer trips with the Royal Flying Doctor Services from outlying communities, and that alone would save a lot of money.

The people here were willing to help and to give generously and in turn she was obliged to do everything she could to show them she respected that. Staying here in Lewisville, settling down and marrying Geoffrey, was probably the right thing to do.

Ruby sighed again, this one more heavy than the last. She stood and walked to the rail, hugging the post that went all the way up to the veranda roof.

'The right man is out there for you, Ruby Valentine,' Viola said, as though she could feel Ruby's internal struggle. 'There's no need to doubt that.'

'But how do I *know*, Vi?' Her words were vehement.

Viola grinned and shrugged. 'You just do. Like Cameron did with Hannah. Like I did with Bill. Just don't go closing off your mind too soon. There's still so much to happen in your life, my Ruby, more experiences for you to have, but whatever you choose, I have the feeling you'll do just fine.'

Ruby looked down the street, in the direction Hamilton had gone, unable to stop thinking about the way he made her feel. 'I hope so,' she whispered.

Hamilton was enjoying working in Lewisville. He'd been ready for a change of pace and after settling himself into Brandon's unit, he knew that being here in the Outback was exactly what he'd needed. Being here, helping out his family, was good. The fact that he was learning more about his own family heritage was a bonus.

He could easily recall the summer he'd spent here, running around with Brandon, playing a lot of football. That had been all he could think about back then. Playing professional football, and now that Ruby had jogged his memory, he could even remember the time when he and Brandon had been determined to see how far they could kick a football, but as there had been an under-eights game being played on the oval they hadn't had goalposts. Both of them had begged Ruby to stand at the other end of the street where they'd been playing, with her arms up straight above her head.

Hamilton smiled, unable to believe he'd actually seen a flicker of interest dash in and then quickly out of Ruby's eyes. He'd admired her spunk in turning them down and soon he and Brandon had turned their attention to something else. Back then, Ruby had just been another girl who lived at Viola's place because of the teen shelter. Ruby had tragically lost her parents and needed help. That had been all, and then later when she'd started to become more like a family member, Hamilton had simply viewed her the way he viewed Lorelai, the girl who had grown up with them in Oodnaminaby, who had always been like a surrogate sister. Ruby had been no different…until the night before he'd been due to leave Lewisville and return to Ood.

The night when Ruby had tried to kiss him.

He was fairly sure Ruby had thought he'd forgotten all about it and back then he'd been incredibly flattered but she'd been just a lonely, mixed-up kid.

Not so now.

He'd also discovered on his first night in town, when he'd retreated to the pub after realising he had a strong desire to kiss her, that Ruby was indeed dating Geoffrey. Strange. The two of them seemed completely incompatible—but that was just his opinion. The fact that the woman could turn his insides into knots had nothing to do whatsoever with his rationalisation.

'Ruby.' He breathed her name as he stood in the small kitchenette of the medical practice, waiting for the coffee-machine to finish dripping.

'Yes?' she answered, walking into the room, and Hamilton quickly snapped his thoughts back to the present. 'Did you want me for something?'

Hamilton turned to look at her and immediately clamped his jaw, his eyes quickly drifting over her beautiful body before shaking his head. He was lying, of course, because ever since his first night here he'd done nothing but dream of Ruby, dream of holding Ruby close, dream of pressing his lips to her perfectly shaped mouth. Did he want her for something? That was a loaded question.

He quickly lowered his gaze, unable to meet her eyes, but realised his mistake too late as his sluggish mind computed what she was wearing. For the past few days she'd been dressed in either three-quarter pants or linen shorts that came to just above her knee; cotton shirts that seemed to sculpt her curves to perfection; and her glorious dark hair pulled back into a no-nonsense but functional ponytail. She wore little to no make-up, her lips now covered with a light sheen of gloss, making them seem good enough to kiss. For years he'd known she was beautiful, he'd accepted that as fact, but today…she was rocking him senseless.

Today, as the temperature was due to hover somewhere between thirty-seven and forty degrees Celsius, Ruby had chosen to drive him to the brink of insanity by wearing a soft cotton dress that came to mid-thigh, revealing a generous amount of her smooth, tanned legs. The material was a deep burgundy, printed with small pink and green flowers and buttoned down the front. If it wasn't enough that she'd worn a dress, she'd also changed her hairstyle, somehow bundling it up onto her head in a sort of messy bun with wisps of delicate brown tendrils floating down around her long, smooth neck. Was it any wonder he was having trouble thinking? It was all he could do not to let his jaw drop open and his tongue roll out onto the floor. Ruby Valentine was one incredibly sexy woman. That he could no longer deny.

The other thing that made her look different today was the fact she was wearing glasses, small rectangular frames sitting on her nose, perfecting her classic features.

'Everything OK?' she asked, her tone crisp and clear.

'I…uh…' He stopped and cleared his throat, unable to believe his voice had sounded so husky. 'I didn't know you wore glasses.'

Ruby held his gaze for a fraction of a second longer before turning to reach for her coffee cup. 'Some days the dry heat combined with the air-conditioning really dries out my eyes so I give them a break from having to wear contacts.'

'Oh. OK. How long have you needed to wear glasses?'

'Final year of medical school. I think the strain on my eyes just became too much and I was getting tired all the time and a friend suggested getting my eyes checked and, well…' She trailed off, shrugging one shoulder and pointing to her face. 'These were the result.'

'They suit you. You look very pretty.'

'Oh.' She glanced up at him quickly, suddenly embarrassed. 'Thanks.'

'You're welcome.'

Silence fell as they both turned and looked desperately at the coffee-machine, willing it to hurry up and finish. Time ticked on. Neither of them spoke. Awkwardness seemed to descend on them like a thick, scratchy blanket. Ruby tried to search her thoughts for something to say—*anything* to say—but all she kept coming up with was that Hamilton thought she looked pretty in her glasses. *He thought she was pretty!* She had no idea why that seemed to please her and make her nervous at the same time but it did. Even if he was just saying it to be polite, even if he only meant it in a family sort of way with no other emotion attached, he'd still said it. Hamilton thought she was pretty.

They both stood there. Empty cups in their hands, eyes glued to the excruciatingly slow coffee-machine. Waiting.

When it finally clicked and the light turned green, indicating the coffee was now ready, they both reached for it. Hamilton just beat her to the punch.

'Here,' he said, holding the coffee pot towards her cup.

'Oh. Thanks.' He filled her mug, then his own. Glad of something to do, Ruby took the milk from the fridge and added a splash whilst Hamilton scooped one sugar into his cup. She had the milk, he had the sugar. Was that good? Was that a sign? Were they opposites or were they each other's halves?

Shaking her head over her ridiculous thoughts, she was almost jubilant when she heard the old bell over the front door to the clinic tinkle, indicating someone had just walked in.

'Ah. Work,' she said, before quickly turning and hurrying from the room, careful not to spill her coffee.

After she'd gone, Hamilton stopped stirring his drink and pressed both hands to the small bench, leaning forward as he sucked in a deep, controlling breath. 'Just family. Just friends. Just colleagues. Nothing more. Got it?'

A moment later he straightened up, squared his shoulders, picked up his coffee and walked purposefully to his consulting room, determined to be professional and keep all unwanted thoughts about irresistible Ruby Valentine out of his mind.

CHAPTER FIVE

AT THE end of his first week there, Hamilton felt as though he was starting to find his feet. He'd been out every night for dinner, just as Viola and May had predicted. Last night, though, he'd been back at Viola's and on that occasion Geoffrey, Ruby's boyfriend, had been there. At first Hamilton felt like he'd been hit with a full dose of the green-eyed monster but as he'd watched the two of them together, Geoffrey with his easy politeness and Ruby with her calm indifference, he knew instinctively the match would never last.

With his older brothers falling in love and settling down, he'd seen what two people in love were supposed to look like, and he simply didn't get that sense with Geoffrey and Ruby. It was clear Geoffrey was more hooked on Ruby than she was on him, and as the night progressed, he actually started to feel sorry for the policeman.

Even when they'd met years ago, Geoffrey, a

troubled teen who thanks to Viola and Bill had managed to turn his life around, had been an easy-going and uncomplicated man. While Hamilton had been preparing for his final year of high school, Geoffrey had been accepted to the police academy.

Now, so many years later, it was clear that Geoffrey was indeed a good man, the 'what you see is what you get' type, but he clearly wasn't the right man for Ruby. No. Hamilton shook his head. Ruby needed a man who would challenge her, force her to step outside her very comfortable comfort zone and take chances, make mistakes and really grasp the most out of life.

Someone like...him? As soon as the thought entered his mind, he rejected it. He wasn't here looking for a relationship. In fact, after what he'd been through with Diana, he definitely didn't want to start something with Ruby he knew he wasn't going to finish. He wasn't looking for *that* type of adventure.

The town was abuzz with talk of the bush dance on Saturday night. Every patient who came to see him talked of little else except their excitement, bringing back memories of when he had last attended a Lewisville bush dance. The fact that they'd also be raising money so the clinic could buy some much-needed equipment was a bonus.

'We have bush dances every three months now,' Viola told him on Saturday afternoon as he climbed a ladder to help attach twinkle lights to the outside of the buildings in Main Street. 'Once we all twigged that we can use them not only as a means of getting everyone together, especially as our community is spread so far and wide, but that we can raise funds for whatever needs doing, the council decided to hold them more regularly.' Viola unlooped the next strand of lights from where she'd coiled them around her neck and passed them up to him. 'We've not only raised money for the clinic but we've also built a new room onto the primary school. We've built the helipad and the buildings next to it and we were also able to buy the ambulance.' She sighed with pride. 'It's a great feeling when we all can work together to help—'

'Viola? Viola?' someone called, and Viola quickly turned round to see who needed her assistance.

'Oh, dear. Looks as though I'm needed elsewhere. That's the problem with being on the organising committee. You're always in demand.' Viola looked up the street and saw her surrogate daughter walking towards them, carrying a large box of decorations. 'Oh, Ruby. Just in time. Come and help Hamilton string up these lights.' Without another word Viola lifted the lights from her shoulders and placed them over Ruby's head. 'Thanks, gorgeous girl,' she said, and hurried off to fix whatever problem had arisen.

Hamilton looked down the ladder at where Ruby stood, lights draped around her shoulders, large box in her hands. 'I can probably manage if you have other things to do,' he offered, but she merely shrugged, the lights lifting up and down as she moved, before putting the box down at her feet.

'It won't take long.'

'OK, then.' He returned his attention to hammering in nails, which would anchor the twinkle lights in place. What he didn't need to focus on was the generous amount of leg Ruby was showing off. The denim shorts she was wearing were far shorter than the ones she wore to clinics. He also didn't need to focus on the way the

T-shirt clung to her curves or the way her hair was piled beneath the large bush hat she wore, giving him a clear picture of her glorious, soft neck. The thought of kissing that neck, his lips on her skin, her fresh sunshiny scent drugging his senses until both of them could experience the release—

Stop. Just hammer the nail, he told himself. And don't hit your thumb. No sooner had he had the thought than he missed the nail and hit his thumb.

'Ow.'

'Hit your thumb?' she asked.

'Yep.'

'Are you OK?'

'Yep.' He slid the hammer into the belt loop of his jeans and put his hand out for the next group of lights that needed to be attached. Ruby handed them up to him, a smile on her face. 'What's so funny?' he asked, his tone gruff.

'You are.' Ruby shook her head. 'I was just thinking about that January you spent here. You and Brandon, when you finally took a brief break from playing football, decided to build a billy—'

'Kart.' They spoke the last word in unison.

Hamilton nodded, his smile wide. 'I'd forgotten about that. You remember far more about my summer here than I do.'

Ruby shrugged as he came halfway down the ladder, looking directly into her eyes. She wished she'd had the forethought to wear her sunglasses but she'd left them at home. The way he was looking at her, giving her his undivided attention… She glanced away for a moment, determined to get complete control over her faculties. 'It was the best summer I'd ever had. I know that probably sounds terrible given my parents had died only a few months before, but for the first time in my life I knew I didn't have to move. I could stay in one place for an extended period of time. I could make *real* friendships and know that the following day I wouldn't have to pack everything up and move simply because my parents had heard of another great means of getting rich quick. It was my very first Christmas, my first New Year, my first summer holidays spent in one place.'

'Everything was so new to you, I guess it's only natural that you remember it all so clearly.'

'Exactly, and that's why I can remember the billy kart and being pressured to be a human goalpost and experiencing my first Outback bush dance.'

'It was my first one, too. In fact, it's been my only one. This one will be my second.'

'We stuck together, both of us unsure what was going on.'

'That's right, and I think we danced at least fifty per cent of the dances together.' His smile was wide and bright.

'Because that way we wouldn't have to be embarrassed if we—'

'Stepped on each other's feet,' they said together, then laughed.

'It was a good night. I really enjoyed myself.'

Ruby was pleased to hear that and she wondered if he really did remember what had happened afterwards. Knowing there was nothing she could do to change the past, she decided to be brave and address the issue. 'And then I had to go and ruin it.' She tried to say the words matter-of-factly, to be nonchalant and appear that she didn't really mind what her fifteen-year-old self had gone and done.

'How did you ruin it?' he asked, coming down the last few rungs on the ladder so they were at a more even height. Ruby looked up at him, just as she'd done that night. Her gaze flicked from his eyes to his mouth and suddenly her bravery seemed to vanish. She breathed out, trying to keep her heart rate at a normal pace. The way he was looking at her now was the way he'd looked at her on his first night back in Lewisville, when they'd been in the clinic…the two of them… close…private…intimate.

She needed to break the moment, to get them back onto a more comfortable footing as they had been only moments before. Oh, why had she even brought the subject up? It was clear he didn't remember the way she'd made a complete fool of herself so why had she even bothered to address it? *Too late now,* her brain was telling her erratic heartbeat.

'How did I—?' She stopped and cleared her throat and decided if she perhaps just blurted it out, the uncomfortable moment would end and they could put this awkwardness behind them once and for all and just be two colleagues who were slightly friends and were working together for a while. Ruby exhaled harshly. 'Because I tried to kiss you. Remember? After the dance had ended? We went back to Vi's house and—'

Hamilton blinked once, the smile now small on his lips. Small and a little bit intimate. 'I remember, Ruby.'

'You do!' She was surprised at that. 'Oh. Well. Anyway, that's how I, um…ruined what was otherwise one of the happiest nights of my life.'

'I don't think you ruined it at all.'

Ruby covered her face with her hands, her embarrassment getting the better of her. 'Can we please not talk about it? Just drop the subject.'

'Why?' Hamilton reached out and pulled her hands away from her face, holding them for a moment. Ruby looked at their hands then back to him, becoming more confused with each passing moment. 'From what I can remember, we'd had a great night, we'd danced, we'd laughed and when we went to Vi's, you stood outside your bedroom door and gave me a hug to say thanks.'

'And then I rested my hands on your chest.' She put her hands on his chest as she spoke, re-enacting the scene.

'Then you slid them up around my neck, looking at me with those big green eyes of yours, your lips parted enticingly.' Ruby didn't put her hands around his neck. She couldn't because she knew what would happen if she did. He would remove them. He would take a step back and reject her. 'My hands were still around your waist from the hug we'd shared.' He placed his hands on her waist, the lights still hanging around her neck clicking a little as they both shifted closer. The touch of his hands on her body caused her insides to flood with instant heat and her heart was now racing a mile a minute.

'Then you looked at me.'

'I did.'

'Then you removed my hands from your neck and rejected me.' Ruby clenched her jaw, surprised that after all these years the hurt was still there. She immediately dropped her hands and stepped back, severing the contact with him, rejecting *him*. 'You didn't want to kiss me and that's fine. I was just a stupid girl with a her first real teenage crush and I know you didn't find me attractive and—'

'What are you talking about? You were a knockout, you still are. Saying no to you was incredibly difficult, Ruby, but I couldn't take advantage of you.'

'What?' She looked up at him.

'Only a few months before, you'd lost your parents. That's incredibly traumatic, Ruby. You were starting a new life here in Lewisville and, besides, a lot of the time with the teenagers who came to Viola and Bill for help, they often only stayed for a few months—six at most—before moving on. How was I to know, if I'd kissed you, whether I'd ever see you again? How was I to know I wasn't some guy you were testing out your new moves on? I was due to leave the next day to return to Oodnaminaby, where I was about to start my last year of high school. Edward was putting pressure on me to study, I wanted to quit and play professional football and he later admitted that he initially sent me here hoping Bill would knock some sense into me.' Hamilton pushed a frustrated hand through his hair.

'I'd always been good friends with Brandon and it was fantastic to come and spend some time here, being free, being a typical teenage boy, in a house where there was one mother and one father and the epitome of normalcy. And then you walked into the room. I remember the first time I met you, Ruby. I was stuffing my face with the incredible cakes Viola had baked and when you walked in, I looked up and thought you were the most beautiful girl I'd ever seen. Then I choked on my mouthful.'

Ruby shook her head. 'I don't… I don't remember that.'

'You were wearing flip-flops, a peach-coloured skirt and a lime-green top.'

'Obviously I also had no dress sense,' she remarked with a slight smile.

'Your dark hair was short and a little spiky on top. You slipped on a pair of sunglasses and basically walked out your bedroom door, through the house, past Brandon and I and out the front door.' Hamilton pointed to her long hair piled beneath her hat. 'I like your hair long. It suits you better.'

'Oh.' She touched the back of her neck, feeling highly self-conscious with all the compliments he was giving her. 'Thanks. I always hated having short hair.'

'Really?'

She nodded. 'My mother used to say it was much easier to manage, that I didn't have time to be fussing with long hair when we were usually underground in a mine surrounded by dirt, so as soon as it reached my shoulders, she'd cut it short. I was astonished when Vi said it was fine with her if I wanted to grow my hair.' Ruby shrugged. 'Just another one of those small areas where I'd started to realised I'd always led an abnormal life.'

Hamilton slowly shook his head at her words. 'It can't have been easy for you and I'm truly sorry if you thought I was rejecting you that night, Ruby, but in a way I guess I was. In my own mind, however, I knew I couldn't kiss you because it would be a violation of trust. You were a girl still grieving, still adapting to the changes in your life, and the last thing you would have needed was a romantic entanglement. Kissing you wouldn't have been fair—to either of us.'

'Chivalry,' she said, nodding.

'Yup. Blame my brothers for knocking it through my thick skull.'

'And all these years I thought you'd thought I was ridiculous and foolish and—'

'No.' He cut off her words.

Ruby stood there and stared at him, glad she'd

raised the subject, glad he'd taken the time to explain his side of the story. Neither of them moved, the intensity that had previously existed as a small spark all those years ago now growing at a rapid rate between them.

Knowing she should say something to change the mood, to break the moment, Ruby racked her brains but was unable to come up with a normal, natural topic of conversation. So she continued to stand there, staring into his bright blue eyes. They were a deeper shade of blue than Brandon's, with little flecks of yellow and green here and there. His nose was a little crooked, indicating it had been broken at some point in the past, although right now she wasn't able to think when that might have happened.

Somewhere up the street someone dropped something loud and heavy. Both Ruby and Hamilton turned to look, effectively breaking the bubble they'd been enclosed in. It was only then that Ruby remembered they were standing in Main Street, in a *busy* Main Street, with many people about, and she'd been struck so dumb by her conversation with Hamilton that she'd forgotten that *anyone* could have been watching them.

She glanced surreptitiously around but everyone seemed completely engrossed in whatever it was they were doing. She breathed a sigh of relief and closed her eyes, silently berating herself for once more being completely hypnotised by Hamilton Goldmark. Would she ever learn?

Then again, he'd just called her beautiful. It wasn't every day a man told her she was beautiful. Even at fifteen he'd thought she was beautiful, and if he'd told her that back then, he would have been the first boy ever to have said such a thing to her. She wished he had.

'Uh… Well… We…' Hamilton pointed up the ladder.

'Yeah. Right.' Ruby nodded but as they moved, the wind picked up a little and the next moment Ruby blinked. 'Argh.'

'What's wrong?' Hamilton was instantly concerned.

'Nothing. Just…something in my eye.'

'That's not nothing and you know it, Ruby. Removing a foreign object from an eye can be very—'

'Oh, shut up and look, will you?' she growled,

and Hamilton found it hard to repress a smile at her impatience.

'OK. Head up.'

She did as she was told.

'Get your hands out the way, Ruby.' He moved them lightly away from her face. 'I can't see with your gargantuan baseball-mitt hands in the way.'

'Oi! I do not have—'

'Quiet, please. I can't concentrate with you yammering on,' he interjected as he stepped closer, putting his hand to her face and tilting her head up a little higher. Carefully, he spread her eyelid wide, noting her eye was already starting to stream. 'Ah. I see it. There's the offending little UFO.'

'I don't have a UFO in my eye,' she replied, trying desperately to ignore the way his extremely close proximity appeared to be setting her entire body on fire.

'Unidentified foreign object. Still. Stay still, Ruby,' he scolded, his voice dipping to an almost whisper. 'Fair dinkum, you're a bad patient. Almost… There!'

He withdrew his hands and eased back just a little. 'It was quite a big bit of grit.' He held out his finger so she could examine the offender. Ruby blinked and wiped at her eye, then put her hands around Hamilton's wrist, turning his arm a little so she could see it better.

'Huh. Stupid thing,' she whispered.

'So small yet it can cause so much pain,' he returned, his voice equally as low as he looked down into her upturned face.

Ruby knew she should drop her hands, should step back, should put some much-needed distance between Hamilton and herself, but right at this moment she didn't appear capable of doing anything other than moving her watery gaze from his eyes back to his lips, wondering just how it might feel to have them pressed against her own.

'Ruby?' At the sound of Geoffrey's voice, Ruby jerked back, dropping her hold on Hamilton's arm and shifting away from him. She couldn't go far, though, as she still had a set of twinkle lights around her neck. Hamilton bent down to pick up the other end of the lights, making her look like a dog on a leash.

'Yes?' she answered, as Geoffrey crossed to her side.

'Are you all right?'

'Yes. Fine. I just...er...had something in my eye but, uh...Hamilton managed to get it out.' She had no idea why she felt so guilty telling Geoffrey this. It had all been harmless, innocent. The removal of a foreign object from an eye. Nothing more. Yet as she dabbed at the corner of her eye again, she knew she was lying to herself. If Geoffrey hadn't interrupted them, and if they hadn't been standing in the middle of the town, and if they'd been all alone as they'd been the first night Hamilton had arrived in town, and if she'd been pressed up against the receptionist desk again, and if he'd been leaning over her just as he had before, his lips again hovering so incredibly close to hers...and if they hadn't also been interrupted that time, then...*yes*. They more than likely would have kissed. The knowledge, the realisation that she would have followed through on the kiss was enough to make her head spin, let alone be assailed by a healthy dose of guilt. She was dating Geoffrey and when a girl was dating a man, she didn't go around almost kissing other men, especially if the man in question was Hamilton.

'Oh. Right. Good thing Hamilton was here, then.' Geoffrey nodded and Ruby realised there wasn't a jealous bone in the man's body. She should be happy about that, shouldn't she? It meant that Geoffrey trusted her. That was good, right?

Hamilton started up the ladder again, the strand of lights in his hand, the other end still slung loosely around Ruby's neck. 'Come on, Ruby. Back to the grindstone,' he teased, giving the lights a gentle tug, urging her a little closer.

'I'll let you get back to it,' Geoffrey said, then looked around to see Joan waving in their direction. 'Oh, it looks as though Joan needs help.' And with that, Geoffrey headed over towards the clinic receptionist.

'He really likes you,' Hamilton stated.

'Geoffrey? Of course he likes me. Geoffrey likes everyone.'

'No. I mean *really* likes you.'

Ruby sighed heavily. 'I know.'

'You don't sound too thrilled about it. Are you trying to get rid of him? Break it off?'

'What? No,' she retorted.

'So you're happy dating him?'

'Oh, stop it, Hamilton.'

'Hey,' he said as he hammered in another nail,

'I'm just asking a question.' Because in his experience women who were happily dating another man didn't look at him the way Ruby had. Hamilton wasn't the type of guy to encroach on an attached woman. *But you did with Diana.* The words popped into his head unbidden and he immediately felt bile rise in his throat. He'd had no idea when he'd started to date his A and E supervisor that she was married. He'd been the adventurous type and so had Diana, but Diana's sort of adventure had been to play around on her estranged husband and as she'd been new to that hospital, no one had had any idea of her true marital status.

No, if Ruby was one hundred per cent certain that Geoffrey was the right man for her, that she loved him and was intent on marrying and spending the rest of her life with the police officer, he would definitely keep his distance.

'I don't see it.' It wasn't until he'd said the words that he'd realised he'd spoken out loud.

'I beg your pardon?' The four words were said slowly and with carefully enunciated precision.

He shrugged. He'd done it now. 'You and Geoffrey. I just don't see it.'

'Then open your eyes. I like Geoffrey. I always have.'

'And you want to spend the rest of your life with him?' Hamilton took the hammer from his belt loop and started banging in another nail.

'That,' Ruby fumed, when he'd finished hammering the nail, 'is none of your business.' With that, she unlooped the lights from around her neck, her eyes starting to blaze with an intensity that made the colour so vibrantly green. She put the lights on the ground and stormed off.

Hamilton tried not to smile as he tugged on the lights, causing them to tangle. Ruby was incredibly dynamic when she was riled up, and as he climbed down the ladder to untangle the lights, he realised the small delay in his task was worth it as the memory of those green eyes, glaring at him with such intensity, was a memory worth holding onto.

CHAPTER SIX

BY THE time night fell, the rains and the setting of the sun provided a bit of cooling relief from the soaring temperatures of the day. Ruby stood in front of the mirror, fussing with her outfit. It was so unlike her to care so much about what she wore. Everyone in this town knew exactly who she was, knew her story and had been immensely proud when she'd returned from completing her medical training to becoming a full-time member of the Goldmark Family Medical Practice.

They'd seen her at her worst and her best and throughout it all, they hadn't cared one jot what she wore. She was neat and professional when she attended clinic, casual but tidy when she made her three-day-long house-call rounds of the surrounding districts, and classically comfortable when she was off duty.

For previous bush dances, she'd worn cowboy boots, with denim jeans and a checked cotton shirt, hair in plaits and her bush hat. Some girls, though, would wear pretty skirts or dresses and as she stood and looked at herself in the mirror, her hair piled on top of her head in a neat bun, her smooth white cotton shirt hanging out over her calf-length twirly skirt, she felt like she was about to head to work.

Twirling a little, she liked the way the skirt flowed around her legs and no doubt it would look great when she was dancing. She peered closer and looked at her face, wondering if she should apply a little more make-up than usual. Some eye shadow as well as mascara? What about some blush? Or bronzer?

'Oh. This is stupid.' Ruby covered her face with her hands. 'Why are you like this? You're not a girly-girl. You never have been. You don't care about fashion or make-up. You don't care what people think of you. You're Ruby Valentine. A respected and loved member of this community. Why are you flipping out like this?'

She sighed and dropped her hands, staring at her reflection, honesty in her eyes. 'You are such a fool. He's just a man. He doesn't care what you wear or how you look. You're dating Geoffrey and Geoffrey likes you just the way you are.'

With that she turned and pulled off the clothes she was wearing, throwing them on the bed and collecting her jeans and checked shirt. 'Nothing's different. Everything's the same. Hamilton's helping out Brandon. You're working with him to help out Brandon. You *can* put up with him for the next five months and three weeks and maybe, just maybe, Brandon will come to his senses earlier and come home, then Hamilton will leave and things can return to normal.' Ruby continued to mutter to herself as she yanked on her cowboy boots. 'Why are guys so sensitive anyway? So Lynn breaks his heart. That's no reason to go off and leave me with Hamilton,' she continued as she wrenched the hairbrush through her hair before roughly plaiting it.

'This whole situation is ridiculous. You've known Hamilton for years.' She took her bush hat from the post of her dresser and put it on her head. She eyed her reflection once more. *And he thought you were beautiful back then.*

Learning that Hamilton hadn't really rejected her, that he'd *wanted* to kiss her that night, had been a revelation. For a start, it had helped her to let go of the antagonism she'd carried towards him and to start seeing him for the man he was today, rather than the boy he'd been back then. Yes, he'd broken her heart, there was no changing that, but now that she understood the real reason he hadn't kissed her, she appreciated him all the more.

'Which is exactly what you don't want to do!' she scolded her reflection. Then, with a firm nod, she stalked to her door, almost jumping in fright when she found Vi standing on the other side, hand raised as though she'd been about to knock. Viola jumped, then clutched her hands to her chest.

'Oh, Ruby, you startled me.'

'Sorry, Vi. Ready?' Ruby's tone was subdued.

'Yes. Ruby? Is something wrong?'

Ruby stopped and forced herself to take a deep breath, letting it out slowly. 'No.' She smiled at Vi. 'I'm fine. You look lovely.'

'As do you, dear.' Viola walked down the corridor and Ruby noticed Vi looking into her room at the mess of clothes all over the place but thankfully she didn't comment on it. As the dance was taking place outside in the street, almost right outside their front door, loud, raucous laughter filled the air.

'Sounds as though it's going to be a bonza night!' Viola said as they both smiled and headed outside.

Ruby walked alongside Vi, smiling brightly and waving at people but not stopping until her gaze settled on...Hamilton. It wasn't until she found him that she realised she'd been unconsciously looking for him.

'Oh, he looks handsome tonight,' Viola said as Hamilton waved, excused himself from Ned Finnegan and headed in their direction. 'He'd give any woman the thrill of adventure.'

'Vi!' Ruby glanced at Vi before returning her gaze to watch Hamilton's long strides.

Viola giggled. 'Hey. I call 'em like I see 'em and I see that he's good for you, my Ruby.'

'Good for me? What do you mean? What are you talking about?' Ruby tried not to watch him, the way he seemed to saunter through the crowd as though he didn't have a care in the world. He was dressed much the same as every man there, with his dark denim jeans, boots and bush hat, but where the others wore checked shirts, Hamilton was wearing a chambray shirt, the colour seeming to highlight his eyes and make them appear brighter—or was it the twinkle lights that gave them that effect?

Before Hamilton reached her side, Ruby felt someone touch the small of her back and she turned around, almost surprised to find herself face to face with Geoffrey.

'You look lovely,' he whispered close to her ear. Ruby smiled at him and took in his uniform.

'Thank you. You're on duty?'

He nodded. 'Thought it best if Ian had the night off to spend with his family. Good for those who are thinking of causing trouble to visibly see there's a police presence here.'

Ruby nodded. 'Good thinking, although it looks as though everyone might be on their best behaviour tonight.' As she spoke, Hamilton finally reached them, having been stopped several times as people shook his hand and greeted him warmly. She'd had no idea he was considered a celebrity. 'Hi.' She beamed brightly.

'Hi, yourself.' He winked at Ruby then took his hat from his head and bent to kiss Viola's cheek.

'You both look like beautiful Outback sheilas,' he drawled, his gaze encompassing them both. He nodded to Geoffrey and proffered his hand. 'G'day, Geoff. Good to see a police presence. Keeping those ruffians in line, eh?'

Geoffrey grinned and shook Hamilton's hand. 'That's my job, buddy.'

Hamilton agreed. 'And I've heard this week that you're very good at protecting this town, along with Ian, of course.'

Geoffrey frowned, a little suspicious. 'Who's been saying stuff?'

'Stuff?' Hamilton eased back on his heels and thought for a moment, twirling his bush hat in his hands. 'Let's see, there was Mrs Mandocicelli who told me how you'd solved the mystery of her missing petunias from her hothouse—young teenagers who were sweet on each other, stealing the flowers to give to each other as an undying token of their love. Classic.' He nodded. 'Then there was Albert Eddington, who couldn't speak highly enough of the way you rescued him from his ute, just before it exploded, and then, of course, there's dear Miss Sommerton over there...' Hamilton smiled and waved at the eighty-seven-year-old woman. 'She told me you'd rescued her cat from a drain the other day—and just in the nick of time, before it started to pour down with rain.' Hamilton nodded, his tone sincere. 'You're definitely a hero in these parts.'

Geoffrey was shrugging his shoulders and shuffling his feet a little. 'Thanks.'

Hamilton laughed, shoved his bush hat back on his head and slapped Geoffrey on the shoulder. 'Come on, hero of Lewisville. I'll buy you a beer—er, light beer, of course. We're both on duty.'

'Make it an orange juice,' Geoffrey said, and a moment later the two men walked off. Ruby stood there gaping for a moment, unsure why she felt so miffed all of a sudden. Why hadn't Hamilton paid her more attention? Hadn't he found her attractive? If she'd worn the dress, would he have stayed?

'It's nice to see the two of them renewing their friendship. The summer when Hamilton was here, the age gap of four years was quite big. Now, though, here they are. Both successful in their chosen fields, both handsome. It warms my heart,' Viola remarked, then turned and waved at Miss Sommerton, before excusing herself to go and speak to the lovely old lady.

'And then there was one.' Ruby sighed, her gaze drawn to where Geoffrey and Hamilton stood at the makeshift bar. The main street of the town had been closed off and an area had been marked out with a hay-bale boundary for dancing. The bush band was still doing its final sound checks and getting ready to not only provide much of the musical entertainment for the evening but also to call out the instructions for the various dances. She watched as the two men lifted their drinks as one of them gave a toast, then Geoffrey drank from his cup of orange juice while Hamilton turned and faced her direction, holding his bottle of sparkling water up in salute to *her*.

Ruby ground her teeth together at his audacity and with that she turned and walked off, mingling with the large crowd.

Hamilton watched her until he could no longer see where she'd gone and wondered if he hadn't overdone things a bit. He'd been able to feel her gaze on him, had been aware that she'd been miffed when he'd headed off with Geoffrey.

How he could sense her moods he had no idea but the thought of riling her a little, teasing her, definitely suited his mood. Even thinking about her marrying Geoffrey, spending her whole life here in this town… He shook his head. He just didn't see it. And he didn't want to see it. He pulled the bush hat further onto his head and listened with half an ear to what Geoffrey was saying, Hamilton's gaze searching the crowd for any sign of Ruby.

Finally he found her, laughing and smiling with Parker, the town's mechanic, who was probably the same age as her. A few teenage boys were hanging around, laughing and enjoying themselves, and Hamilton had to admit Ruby had a way with everyone she met. Somehow she seemed to relax them, put them at ease. She was good with them and he knew it was because she'd lived in a home where everyone was welcome. Viola's complete acceptance of people for who they were deep down inside had rubbed off on Ruby.

As the music started and people took to the floor, Hamilton watched the way Ruby moved, laughing and enjoying herself with one of her friends. It was becoming patently obvious to him that he no longer saw Ruby as a distant family member. Instead, when he looked at her, he saw a bright, vibrant woman who somehow seemed to affect his breathing and make his pulse rate skyrocket with just one smile.

Besides, even if he did find her attractive, it didn't mean anything would happen between them. He had plans. Travel. Exploration. Adventure. Those were his goals for the next few years and he knew a woman such as Ruby wouldn't fit into those plans. Or would she?

'Hamilton, why aren't you out there dancing?' Viola scolded as she walked towards him.

'More importantly, why aren't you?' he countered.

Viola looked away and lifted her chin a little. 'No one's asked me.'

'Really? I find that hard to believe.'

'No, it's true. They all think because I'm old that if I dance, I'm going to bust a hip or something.'

'Well, then, perhaps it's best you dance with a doctor who can render immediate first aid.' He smiled, giving her a wink. Hamilton tipped his hat and bowed. 'Cousin Viola, may I have the honour of this dance?'

'You most certainly may, cousin Hamilton.' With that, they headed out to the dance floor, joining in the long progressive dance. After that, Hamilton seemed to always be dancing, with one woman after the next coming to claim him as their partner.

'We weren't sure you could dance,' Mrs Mandocicelli told him. 'No one wants a sloppy partner.'

'Then thank you for the compliment. You take it easy now, Mrs M. You don't want to overdo things.'

She waved away his concern and professed she was fine. Hamilton made a mental note to keep a closer eye on her. Heart conditions could be monitored and treated with ease so long as the patient didn't over-exert themselves.

Throughout all the dances, even the ones where you constantly swapped partners, Hamilton found himself just missing out on dancing with Ruby. However, it was near the end of a dance where the men were in the inner circle and the women progressed their way round the outer circle that he finally found himself face to face with Miss Ruby Valentine.

'Having fun?' he asked, forcing himself to ignore the increase of his pulse the second her hand slid into his.

'Yes. And you?'

'Great.'

They danced on, both feeling a little awkward, waiting for the dance caller to move them on to the next partner, but that didn't happen. 'Here you stay, till the end of the day,' the caller said, and it was then Ruby knew she'd have to work harder to find a topic of safe conversation for the next minute at least. She'd spent most of the evening still annoyed with him for the way he'd snubbed her earlier on and had managed to avoid him as much as possible, wanting to show him she didn't care one iota what he thought. Now that she was in his arms, she knew it wasn't true.

'I like your hat. More suitable than the peaked cap you've been wearing throughout the week.'

'It's one of Brandon's. I didn't think he'd mind.'

'Ah. I thought it looked too well worn to be new.' They shuffled about on the dance floor a bit more before he tugged lightly on one of her pigtails.

'You look really young with your hair like that. Like a teenager again.'

'My hair was short when I was fifteen.'

'I'm trying to give you a compliment.'

'Why?'

'Because it's nice and I'm a nice guy.'

'Hmm.' She looked as though she didn't believe him. 'Well, if I look fifteen again, then you must be a hormone riddled seventeen-year-old, only interested in playing sport and chasing girls.'

Hamilton grinned. 'That sounds about right.'

'Do you still play sport and chase girls?' Ruby tried to make her question sound as carefree as possible but deep inside she was dying to know if there really was a special someone in Hamilton's life. Was he only pretending to want freedom and adventure because a relationship hadn't worked out? Was he running away, coming to Lewisville for the same reason Brandon had left? A relationship gone sour?

She had no idea why it was so important to know but the instant she'd placed her hand into his, her heartbeat had started to pound out of control. It was time she faced facts. No man had ever made her feel the way he did. There was something about Hamilton that seemed to set her heart on fire and make her body tingle with excited delight.

'Not so much sport,' he replied. 'Unless you count the odd bit of sports medicine.'

'Ah, but you still chase the girls, eh?'

'I wouldn't call it chasing, per se.'

'You don't have a special someone?'

There was one brief moment of hesitation and in that moment Ruby saw the tiniest hint of veiled hurt in his eyes. Then as quickly as it had come, it was gone. 'No.'

'Do you date quite regularly?'

He thought about this for a moment. 'It depends on your definition of "quite regularly".'

Ruby tut-tutted and shook her head at him, her dark pigtails flipping over her shoulders. 'Face it, Hamilton. You're a playboy.'

Hamilton laughed. 'Hardly. What doctor has the time?'

'If it's a priority, I'm sure you'd make the time.'

'You forget, I've been travelling, living overseas. That in itself makes it difficult to maintain a relationship.'

'Even though you're surrounded by pretty doctors and nurses?'

He shook his head. 'I have a new rule. I don't date other medics.'

'Aha. There's something in that.' She nodded as though pleased she'd finally managed to put a piece of the puzzle into place. 'What was her name?' she teased, thinking of different ways she could cajole the information out of him.

'Diana.'

His straightforward answer surprised her and when she met his gaze, she realised the veiled pain she'd only glimpsed earlier was back. 'What happened?'

'She was married.' He shook his head, still being completely open and honest with her. Ruby felt like she was prying yet at the same time she really did want to know. 'I had no idea. No one did. She was new to the hospital—Director of A and E. She was filling in while my sister-in-law Darla took maternity leave. We hit it off straight away and she signed on to be my supervisor whilst I completed my diploma in emergency medicine.'

'*She's* the reason you transferred and finished your course in Tarparnii?'

'Yes.'

'I'm sorry, Hamilton.' Ruby shifted a little closer as they continued to dance, Hamilton swaying her around in time with the music, sliding his hand further around her waist. He marvelled at what had just occurred, trying to comprehend it because every time he'd even mentioned Diana's name in the past, his heart had constricted, his brow had furrowed and his breathing had become agitated. Now, though, telling Ruby the bare facts of what had happened to him, of why he was most certainly *not* a playboy, none of those usual things had happened. Why was that? Was he really over Diana once and for all? Was that why it didn't hurt to talk about her?

Or was it because Diana had been replaced in his affections by the woman presently in his arms?

The instant the thought entered his mind, he pushed it away. He'd come to Lewisville for an adventure but not *that* type of adventure. Ruby was a friend. Nothing more. She was also dating another man and, despite how serious it was or wasn't, it had nothing to do with him. At least that's the story his brain was telling. His heart, however…that was another matter entirely and when the music ended, everyone around them clapping their thanks to the band, Hamilton and Ruby stayed where they were. In each other's arms.

They looked at each other in stunned disbelief and while only a second had passed since the music had finished, neither of them seemed in any hurry to move. It took another moment longer before Hamilton stepped back and brought her hand to his lips. 'Thank you for the dance,' he murmured, caressing his thumb over the skin he'd just kissed.

Ruby's heartbeat raced out of control at the gallant gesture and she raised her free hand to her chest, a little overwhelmed. 'Er…' She swallowed over the sudden dryness in her throat. 'You're welcome,' she breathed.

They stood there. Her hand still in his. The world turning around them but neither aware of its existence. Ruby parted her lips to allow pent-up air to escape and slowly slipped her tongue out, wetting her lips. Hamilton's gaze dipped, following the action intently.

'Hamilton?' she breathed, unsure what she was asking, her eyes wide and filled with confusion.

'I know,' he whispered.

Before either of them could say any more, there was a loud noise from their right. Someone screamed and the next second there was an almighty crash. Ruby and Hamilton looked in the direction of the noise then back at each other. Without another word they rushed towards the commotion, people parting for them to get through. It wasn't until they stood beside an unconscious Mrs Mandocicelli, who had collapsed onto one of the refreshment tables, that Ruby realised Hamilton was still holding her hand. She let go so quickly it was as though she'd been burnt.

Ruby turned to see Viola standing close by. 'Get my emergency bag,' she said. Viola nodded then rushed away.

'Mrs M.?' Hamilton called, but received no response. 'She's stopped breathing.'

'Myocardial infarction?' she murmured, and

Hamilton nodded, immediately beginning compressions.

'What's that?' someone nearby asked.

'Heart attack,' Joan responded, as she pushed her way through the crowd. 'What do you need?'

'Get the oxygen from the clinic, then get the ambulance ready,' Ruby responded.

'Geoffrey!' Hamilton called into the crowd. The police officer appeared within a second. 'Clear this crowd and get a chopper or a plane here, stat,' Hamilton ordered.

While they'd been talking, Ruby shifted into position for expired air resuscitation. She pinched Mrs M.'s nose, tilted her head back and secured her chin, before breathing two breaths into her mouth. Hamilton continued with the cardiac compressions.

Everyone was silent, except for Hamilton's voice as he counted out loud to ensure Ruby knew when to breathe into Mrs M.'s mouth, the woman's chest rising and falling as they continued, determined to save her life. By the time Viola came back with the medical bag and Joan returned with the oxygen, it felt as though they'd been working to get Mrs M. breathing for ages when it had, in fact, been just over a minute. They continued to concentrate.

'Come on, Mrs M.,' Ruby whispered near her ear. 'We need you. Come back to us.'

Hamilton's voice continued the count and Ruby breathed two breaths, then checked Mrs M.'s carotid pulse. They'd have to swap soon if—

'It's there! Faint but there!'

Everyone around them applauded and breathed big sighs of relief. Ruby sat back on her heels and closed her eyes for a moment, relief flooding through her. She reached for the oxygen Joan had brought over and together they fitted Mrs M. with a non-rebreather mask, before shifting her carefully onto her side and into the coma position. Joan put a blanket over their patient and knelt down beside Mrs M., continuing to support and monitor her.

'There you go. Rest now,' Hamilton said softly as he stroked the woman's hair. Ruby watched the way he cared, the way he spoke to their patient as though she was someone incredibly important to him rather than a woman he'd known for less than a week. The sight warmed her heart.

Hamilton stood and stretched his arms above

his head, loosening up from the tense situation. Ruby also stood and did the same thing, clasping her hands behind her back and flexing. Their gazes met and held, both of them elated they'd managed to save Mrs M.'s life. That elation was starting to turn into light-headed euphoria so when Hamilton opened his arms wide, inviting her closer, it seemed the most natural thing in the world for her to accept.

CHAPTER SEVEN

RUBY leaned her head against Hamilton's chest and closed her eyes. For one brief moment in her life she felt completely at peace, completely content. His arms were strong and secure, making her feel protected and cherished. She'd been searching for most her life for such a moment as this and even though she'd told herself to give Hamilton a wide berth, she was not only going to accept this moment but enjoy it as well. If only the world could stay like this for ever.

'Well done,' he murmured near her ear.

'You, too,' she replied, lifting her head to look up at him. The instant she looked at him she realised it was a mistake. Being in his arms, staring up into his eyes, feeling the overwhelming sensations of deep attraction flooding her entire being... She swallowed, unable to move.

Hamilton looked into her beautiful face, his gaze flicking to take in her luscious lips. It would take nothing to lower his head the remaining distance, to give them both what they seemed to want. Ruby was in his arms, looking at him as though she wanted nothing more than for him to do exactly that.

Someone behind them cleared their throat and it was then both Ruby and Hamilton became aware of the crowd gathered around them. Although their hug had lasted less than a minute, they both sprang apart and quickly focused their attention on Mrs Mandocicelli.

Hamilton glanced around, his eyes meeting Viola's. The woman was beaming almost from ear to ear. Hamilton quickly looked away. If she'd witnessed that incredibly intense moment between him and her surrogate daughter, she wouldn't be smiling, she'd be frowning—right? She must be happy because they'd been successful in reviving Mrs M.

'Don't struggle,' Ruby said softly as she hooked her stethoscope into her ears and listened to Mrs M.'s chest while Hamilton used the portable sphygmomanometer to check Mrs M.'s blood pressure. 'Everything's OK now. You gave us quite a scare.'

Mrs M. motioned to the oxygen mask, trying to talk. Ruby lifted it, just for a second.

'I took a tablet. It didn't work,' she managed to whisper.

'It doesn't matter now. Hamilton and I will get you sorted out,' Ruby replied. 'Even now your vitals are stronger than a few minutes ago. That's a good thing.' She replaced the mask then stroked Mrs M.'s hair. 'Rest.'

They both continued to monitor her, administering pain relief while Joan fetched the ambulance, driving it as close as possible to their location. When Mrs M. was secured onto the stretcher and inside the ambulance, she insisted that both Hamilton and Ruby go with her.

'I don't like hospitals,' she mumbled, lifting off the oxygen mask from her mouth and nose. 'I need you both there. You will help me to be brave.'

Ruby quickly put the mask back in place then looked at Hamilton, who nodded. 'We want to keep her as calm as possible,' he murmured low enough so their patient couldn't hear.

'Agreed. The last thing we want is for her to get upset.' Even though the last thing *she* wanted was to spend more time in close proximity to Hamilton. The fact that they'd looked into each other's eyes, registering that there really was something electrical happening between them, was reason enough to keep their distance.

'Sometimes things just happen,' Viola had explained to her when she'd been a teenager, asking questions and wanting to know more so she could better understand her past. 'And sometimes bad things happen to good people. Unfortunately, that's a part of life, darling.'

Ruby knew that all too well. Sometimes things did happen out of the blue, such as a mining accident that had not only taken the lives of her parents but had also buried her alive. Such as her thinking she could stay the rest of her life here in Lewisville, content to marry Geoffrey and find a firm grounding in stability. Such as experiencing an overpowering chemistry with a man she wasn't even sure she liked.

Ruby swallowed and tried not to look at Hamilton as Joan drove carefully to the helipad. They rendezvoused with the chopper, Geoffrey overseeing the transfer and ensuring everything was fine.

'We'll leave Lewisville in your capable hands,' Ruby said to Joan and Geoffrey.

'You're both going? Of course,' Geoffrey continued before she could say a word. 'Mrs M. would want both of you there to keep her calm.'

Ruby frowned at Geoffrey's simple acceptance of the situation. Didn't he think it a little strange that they *both* had to go? Wasn't he concerned that she'd once again be alone with Hamilton? Had he even seen the way she and the man beside her had been gazing into each other's eyes? With a mixture of guilt and total confusion Ruby shook her head and turned to climb into the chopper, seating herself near Mrs M.

Hamilton held out his hand to Geoffrey. 'Thanks for your help.' He looked across at Joan and smiled. 'And yours, too. Go and enjoy the rest of the night. Dance. Have fun. We'll keep you informed of Mrs M.'s progress.'

'Thanks,' Joan said, coming to stand next to Geoffrey. Hamilton watched as the pretty paramedic glanced up at the police officer, noticing a deep longing in her eyes. 'I think Geoffrey could definitely do with enjoying a dance or two.'

As Hamilton climbed into the chopper and buckled his seat belt, he wondered whether Geoffrey had any clue that Joan was interested in him. Was it difficult for Joan to see Geoffrey with Ruby? Could Joan see that Ruby and Geoffrey were all wrong for each other, just as he could? As the chopper took off, Hamilton looked at the woman beside him. She was buckled in with a headset on so she could talk and listen to the pilot. She held Mrs M.'s hand, doing everything she could to reassure their patient. She was a good doctor but she could be brilliant if she gave herself half the chance.

He understood that until she'd come to live in Lewisville, she'd never had any sort of stability, but locking herself away, failing to reach her full potential, settling for a second-rate existence when the world was her oyster was almost a travesty.

Perhaps during his time here he could help her to see that. Help her to see that staying here for ever, marrying Geoffrey and starting a family without even thinking of doing any other sort of medical training, was a waste of her life.

Of course, if she were to break up with Geoffrey, it would mean he'd have to re-evaluate things, such as whether he'd take that step back into the ring of romance and try once more to have a successful relationship.

Ruby was not Diana. He knew that. In fact, they were polar opposites but putting his heart out there again, especially with the chance that it might get well and truly trampled on, was a frightening prospect.

At the moment, though, it didn't matter. He respected Geoffrey as well as Ruby but until they'd come to realise the truth, that they weren't meant for each other, she was definitely off limits.

During the short flight to Broken Hill Base Hospital, Mrs Mandocicelli remained in a stable condition and on their arrival was taken to the critical cardiac unit, where staff performed an ECG and arterial blood gases to check if there had been any permanent damage to the heart.

'Everything is looking good,' Hamilton explained to their patient so she didn't get frightened. 'They're going to keep you in for a few days for observation.'

Ruby held Mrs M.'s hand. 'You'll be as right

as rain and back in Lewisville before you know it,' she promised.

'I don't like hospitals much but I know I have to stay.'

'You also have quite a few friends that live around Broken Hill that you don't get to see all that often so no doubt the nurses here are going to be shooing your visitors away so you can find some time to rest.'

Mrs M. brightened at this idea. 'Thank you both for being with me.'

'It's our pleasure,' Hamilton responded, and winked at her. Mrs M. smiled but closed her eyes as the medication she'd been given started to take effect.

'You're such a flirt, young Hamilton.' Mrs M.'s words were slow and a little slurred but still quite audible. 'Such a charmer, just like my late husband.' She smiled and sighed. 'You watch out for him, Ruby. All the girls in the town will be wanting to marry the doctor. You need to protect him.' Mrs M. yawned. 'They all wanted to dance with him and they all want to mar...' Her words trailed off as she slipped peacefully to sleep.

Ruby found it difficult to look at Hamilton,

feeling a little self-conscious at being told to protect the very man she was starting to have feelings for. She busied herself checking the oxygen saturation and the readouts from the ECG machine, ensuring all Mrs M.'s vitals were in order.

Hamilton watched her for a moment before heading to the nurses' station. She was glad of the reprieve from his enigmatic presence. Why was it she felt all young and girly and hormonal around Hamilton? Why couldn't she feel that way around Geoffrey? Ruby closed her eyes for a brief second and sighed. 'Oh, Geoffrey.' In admitting to herself that she had feelings for Hamilton, she not only felt incredibly guilty but also like a big fat liar.

When she'd finally agreed to go out with Geoffrey, he'd been so happy. He'd asked her several times before but each time she'd declined. So what made you accept? She pondered the question, trying to figure it out, and as she sat down in the chair beside Mrs M.'s bed, she started to realise that she hadn't wanted to end up all alone.

First her parents had been taken from her and then seven years ago Bill Goldmark, the man she'd come to look upon as her father, had passed away, too. Last year, Brandon had met Lynn and had shown all the signs of a man wanting to settle down. Viola had had her teen outreach mission and although Ruby was more than happy to assist Vi in any way she could, it certainly wasn't *her* mission.

When Geoffrey had asked her again to consider going out with him, outlining his carefully prepared three-year plan—one year of dating, one year of engagement, one year of marriage before starting a family—Ruby had rationalised that if she didn't accept, she might very well end up on the shelf. At twenty-eight, she realised she wasn't getting any younger and she did care for, respect and admire Geoffrey.

Now, with Hamilton coming back into her life, she'd realised that what she felt for Geoffrey was nowhere near the pulse-racing, heart-stopping excitement she felt for Hamilton. He could wind her up so easily, teasing her, frustrating her, placating her with one of his hypnotic smiles. He just needed to look at her with those bright blue eyes of his and her heart would melt.

She had no idea what the future held, she wasn't even sure if Hamilton really reciprocated her feelings. They were certainly highly aware of each other but that didn't necessarily mean they'd end up spending the rest of their lives together. But what she did know was that it wasn't at all fair to Geoffrey for her to continue dating him. There was no way she could ever marry him and he deserved to be free to find the woman who *was* right for him. 'You need to talk to Geoffrey,' she whispered to herself. 'You need to end it.'

Feeling a little more in control having come to this decision, she looked over her shoulder, wondering what Hamilton was doing. She could see he was at the nurses' station, nodding at something one of the nurses was saying, listening intently to the buxom blonde who appeared to be invading his personal space. The nurse laughed, fluttering her eyelashes at him and putting her hand onto his shoulder, then sliding her fingers down over Hamilton's firm biceps.

Ruby clenched her teeth, realising Mrs M. had been right. Hamilton *was* an incredibly handsome man and all the women knew it. Tonight at the dance every single female over the age of eighteen had ogled Hamilton, eager to be his partner, if only for a short time during the progressive dances. He was becoming the catch of the community. 'Everyone wants to marry a doctor,' she whispered, repeating Mrs M.'s words as she stood and replaced the chair against the wall, out of the way.

She continued to watch him for a moment longer, then started to realise he appeared a little agitated. He stepped back as the blonde reached towards him again and this time he knocked over a chair. Didn't he like the attention he was receiving? He'd certainly been enjoying himself at the dance and although he'd said he wasn't interested in settling down, she was sure he'd change his mind if he met the right woman.

You're the right woman, a little voice inside her head said but she quickly pushed the thought away. No. Hamilton may be handsome and funny and adventurous and exciting but he was also leaving when Brandon returned, moving on to his next adventure. She had to remember that.

It was yet another reason why she shouldn't take the way he made her feel too seriously. Hamilton flirted and charmed every woman he met, regardless of age. Even Mrs M. had called him a charmer and she was right. He had so much charisma, was able to put anyone at ease within a matter of seconds, and when he smiled, looking at you as though you were incredibly special, you *felt* incredibly special. That was exactly the look Ruby could see on the face of the nurses as he smiled and said something to make them all laugh.

'Flirt,' she mumbled, but where Mrs M. had meant it as a compliment, Ruby meant it as an insult, annoyance ripping through her. Why was it necessary for him to flirt with anything in a skirt? Couldn't he stop for just one second? Then again, she wasn't sure he could. When she thought about his older brothers, about the way Hamilton had been raised—*all* the Goldmark men were filled to the brim with good manners and charm. Even Brandon had charm and charisma in spades. She couldn't ask Hamilton to go against the grain but did he have to be so lethal to every woman he met?

Leaning forward to press a kiss to Mrs M.'s forehead, Ruby headed to the nurses' station just as one of the other nurses touched Hamilton's arm. Ruby frowned. He wasn't a piece of meat they could paw any time they felt like it.

'That's so funny. You're an incredibly funny man, Hamilton.'

Hamilton saw Ruby enter the nurses' station and immediately shifted to her side, draping his arm casually about her waist. He turned and looked directly into her eyes. 'Ready to go, hon?'

Hon? Ruby was about to raise her eyebrows when she saw a pleading look in his eyes, begging her to rescue him. So he *hadn't* been leading them on. He'd been trying to escape. Wanting to smirk, wanting to laugh and tease him, she resisted the impulse and instead nodded, leaning into him a little. 'Yes. Mrs M.'s sleeping and in good hands. Let's head home, *hon.*'

She turned and smiled at the nurses, noting the one who had latched onto Hamilton was already disinterested. With another word of thanks, the two of them headed out the ward. When they were clear, Ruby went to move away but Hamilton tightened his arm about her waist.

'Not yet. She might have friends and they'll report back that we were just pretending and—'

Ruby sighed with exasperation, trying not to react to the strong thread of heat pulsing through her entire body at his nearness. 'Fair dinkum,

Hamilton. She's going to find out sooner than you think. Most of the people in this place know me, they know who I am.'

'Yes, but they don't know who *I* am and I promise, if there are any repercussions, I will take full responsibility. Just not tonight.' There was a tiredness to his words and she realised that, all up, it had been an eventful night. Perhaps he was right.

They made their way to the helipad, pleased when the helicopter pilot said he was ready right now to take them back to Lewisville. Only as they went through their pre-flight safety check did Hamilton release his hold on her and it astonished Ruby to realise she felt completely bereft without his touch.

'When we want a lift back, we have to ensure there aren't any other emergency calls,' Ruby informed Hamilton as they buckled their belts. After that, all conversation was reduced to a word here and there as they both wore noise-cancelling headphones with little microphones attached so they could hear what the pilot was saying.

After they'd touched down in Lewisville, then watched as the helicopter took off, Ruby and

Hamilton stood at the edge of the helipad, looking at the night sky.

'I hope the rest of the dance went well,' he murmured. 'Up until the emergency, I was having a great time.'

Ruby took her phone from her pocket. 'You certainly looked the part. Hey, where's your hat? Or should I say Brandon's hat?'

'I took it off when we were attending to Mrs M. Viola picked it up.'

'Oh. Good.'

'Who are you calling?'

'I was going to get Geoffrey to come and pick us up.'

Hamilton shook his head, taking her phone from her and ending the call. 'No need to bother him. It's not far.'

She raised her eyebrows in surprise. 'You don't mind walking?'

He spread his arms wide. 'On a night like this? It's perfect.'

'OK.' Ruby put her phone away. Neither of them spoke as they started walking but for the first time the silence wasn't an uncomfortable one. They'd only been walking for five minutes before Ruby asked, 'Why did you pretend we were an item in front of those nurses?'

'Two of them were coming on to me. Very strongly.' He spread his arms wide. 'I thought you'd be happy to help me out.'

'So you didn't *want* those women ogling you? Why?'

Hamilton rolled his eyes. 'Oh, Ruby, Ruby, pay attention. I'm not in town to find a girlfriend. I'm not ready for that sort of adventure. Besides, after what happened with Diana, I've made it a personal policy not to date my co-workers.'

'Especially if they're your supervisor, right?'

He smiled. 'Right.'

They walked on for half a minute, silence settling around them once more. 'There's more to it than that, isn't there?' she asked after a moment.

'More to what?'

'More to you not dating co-workers.'

Hamilton looked over at her but even though his eyes had adjusted to the dark, he still couldn't see her face too clearly. 'How can you know that?' he asked.

Ruby shrugged. 'I don't know. I just sense it. I'm right, though, aren't I?'

He nodded. 'Yeah.' He didn't immediately expand on the answer and Ruby started to grow a little impatient. The town wasn't that far from the helipad—only a few kilometres, and they'd be there before she knew it. Hamilton was opening up to her, talking to her, sharing with her, and she desperately wanted to know more about the *real* him.

'Well?'

'Ooh. Miss Impatient, are we?'

Ruby sighed heavily and he chuckled but the sound was more hollow, more wistful than his usual deep laughter.

'All right, then.' He dragged in a deep breath, then slowly exhaled. 'I'm…cautious about dating co-workers because…well, because both my parents were medics.'

'I know.'

'They were both doing their job, putting themselves in danger in order to help others.'

'But that's noble.'

'I know, but if only one of them had been a medical professional, the other would have been at home, able to raise us. Edward wouldn't have had to give up his dreams of becoming a surgeon, Peter and Bart wouldn't have had to post-pone their plans and Ben and I would have had a more normal childhood, rather than often hating Edward because he wouldn't let us do what we wanted to do. He had to become a parent over-night, and he was a strict one, too. It took years for Edward and I to find our brotherly footing again, and that was mostly due to him settling down with Honey.'

'At least you *have* family,' Ruby pointed out.

'I know I shouldn't complain or stress, espe-cially when you've had it much worse than I ever did, but sometimes being the youngest drives me insane. My brothers are still so highly protective and even though I'm thirty years old, to them I'm still a lonely, orphaned nine-year-old boy who needs to be taken care of.' He shook his head, then put a hand on her shoulder. 'I'm sorry if my remarks came across as insensitive. I didn't mean them to—'

'No, it's fine,' she quickly assured him, try-ing not to react to the way his simple touch had caused a multitude of sparks to spread through-out her entire body. 'I asked the question, you gave me a truthful answer. It does explain a lot but your parents fell in love and it was only through a sheer natural disaster that they lost their lives. The chances of history repeating itself are fairly slim. Besides, look at the wonderful years they had together. Meeting at that dance and then being separated. Finding each other years later...' Ruby's voice trailed off into the stillness of the night as she realised the story of Hamilton's parents sounded a lot like what had happened to *them*. They'd met when they'd been teenagers, they'd danced together at a bush dance, they'd gone their separate ways and now... had they found each other again?

'And living happily ever after together—even in death,' Hamilton finished. He was about to remove his hand from Ruby's shoulder when she started speaking softly.

'Unlike my parents. Even when they weren't digging for buried treasure or blasting rock from the earth in their hunt for opals or gold, they were always arguing. Which place to go to next? What to buy with the money they'd made? Should they trade in the old van for a newer model that broke down less or should they invest in better tools and equipment?' She slowly shook her head. 'I don't remember them ever agreeing on anything. From the age of seven, they started taking me underground with them, especially when they were mining inland. At eleven, my dad taught me how to scuba dive so I could help carry their equipment. It may all sound lovely and exciting and thrilling but it wasn't. One time, we were underwater so long we almost ran out of oxygen. Another time, when we were in an abandoned mine shaft, there was a small cave-in and my father's foot became stuck. He fractured it in two places.

'I remember asking them when I was about five why I couldn't go to school like the other kids and they'd tell me I'd have much more fun living in the real world, having adventures and striking it rich.'

Hamilton wasn't sure what to say and he didn't want to stop her from talking so he rubbed his hand on her shoulder, letting her know he felt her pain.

'One time, I remember them arguing. My mother was saying they should leave me with her friend in Melbourne and that way they could focus more on prospecting. My father said I was just getting to the age where I was actually helpful, lugging buckets of rock to the surface and handing him tools.' She sighed, her bitter words mixed with a hint of sadness. 'Then came that fateful day when they were prospecting not far from Lewisville. They hadn't found anything for months and I remember them having an argument the night before. My mother wanted to move. My father "felt lucky".'

Ruby stopped walking for a moment and gazed out into the dark night. Hamilton stood before her, both hands on her shoulders, listening intently but wanting to offer as much support as he could because he had the feeling this wasn't something Ruby talked about all that often.

'We were running out of time and usually when we blasted we'd set the charges and head to the surface, but not that day. That day there was the smell of desperation in the air, especially with my parents constantly arguing. Dad set the charges but something went wrong and as we were on our way out of the cavern, the charge went early— at least, that's what I was told.' She shook her head and looked up at Hamilton. 'The last thing I can remember is them arguing as Dad set the charges.'

'And you were buried alive.' As the words he spoke settled over them, Hamilton was struck with the kind of terror and fear he couldn't remember experiencing before. The thought of Ruby being buried in that mine shaft, of being unable to breathe, her face covered in dirt and silt and—

He drew her into his arms, needing to feel her close to him, almost as though he had to reassure himself she was alive. He wanted to offer her comfort for what she'd been through, even though it was so long ago now. 'How long were you down there before they found you?'

'Six hours. I was unconscious for most of it but even after they found me, it took another three hours for them to dig me out, and all that time I just sort of *knew* my parents were dead.'

'Oh, Ruby.' He rubbed his hand up and down her back. 'What you must have gone through.'

'If it hadn't been for Vi and Bill, I would have been...' She shrugged. 'I don't know. More lost than I am.'

'You're lost?' There was the faintest hint of worried concern in his tone as he pulled back to look at her.

Ruby met his gaze, realising belatedly she might have said too much. 'Aren't we all?' she rationalised a moment later.

'Is that why you're dating Geoffrey?'

'What?' Ruby broke away from his hold and stepped back. 'What does that have to do with anything?'

'I don't know but usually, when people are lost, they tend to grasp onto something solid—a person, a place, a way of life—thinking they might somehow find themselves.'

'A way of life? Isn't that what you're grasping onto, Hamilton? Always travelling? Never settling down? Looking for the next adventure?'

He shrugged one shoulder. 'More than likely. I haven't given it much thought. I guess…I was lost and I grasped onto a way of life,' he stated. 'Isn't that what you've done? Grasped onto life in Lewisville? Too scared to let go and leave in case something goes wrong?'

Ruby lifted her chin a little higher, trying not to let his words affect her. 'What if I have? What's wrong with that?'

'Nothing. Nothing at all, if you're happy.'

She glared at him then shook her head and

started walking again. They weren't far from the turn-off that led to the main street of the town. It was now just after two o'clock in the morning, the only sound around them her footsteps on the dirt road. 'But I still can't leave Lewisville.'

'Seriously?' He followed her.

'I owe this town a very big debt. Besides, I couldn't leave Vi or Brandon. I love being a doctor. I loved coming back to Lewisville and joining the family medical practice with Brandon. It was all I'd ever wanted. To follow in Bill's footsteps, to make my surrogate family proud of me, to give something back to the community that took me in and loved me.'

'So that's it, then?' They turned the corner, the road beneath their feet changing from dirt to bitumen. 'You really are going to stay here? Settle down? Marry Geoffrey?' He paused for a moment then swept his free arm in front of him as though announcing the latest headline for a newspaper. 'The doctor and the cop. Lewisville's wedding of the year.'

'Shut up, Hamilton. You're being obnoxious.'

'Me? I'm never obnoxious.'

'Ha!' She took a few more steps, then stopped

and shook her head. 'Why do you do this to me, Hamilton?' She closed her eyes as though trying to block him out.

'Do what?' His voice was closer than she'd thought and when she opened her eyes, she was surprised to find he'd moved.

'Tie me in knots.'

'If it helps…you do the same thing to me,' he murmured, and stepped a little closer. The still-ness of the night surrounded them, binding them together. They were on the edge of the main part of the town and there wasn't a soul in sight. Everything from the bush dance had been cleared away, not a hay bale in sight in the early morning hours. It was just the two of them.

Ruby put both her hands on his chest, swallowing over her suddenly dry throat as she looked up into his eyes. It was still quite dark, the only light around them that of the streetlamp a little way off. They stood, their faces in shadow, unable to read each other's expressions.

Hamilton's hands rested on her hips as though it was the most natural thing to do. Being this close to Ruby, looking down into her upturned face, seemed completely natural. It was wrong but felt so incredibly right.

'Hamilton?' When she looked up at him, she could only see shaded angles but she could feel his breath on her face.

'What about Geoffrey?'

Ruby shook her head then as the darkness made her bold, she gently caressed his cheek. 'He doesn't…thrill me to the bone…the way you do.'

'Ruby,' he whispered. 'You shouldn't say such things.'

'Why not?'

'Because you're still dating Geoffrey. This is… wrong.'

'And yet it feels so right,' she breathed, lacing her fingers through his hair and urging his head slowly down towards hers.

CHAPTER EIGHT

HAMILTON closed his eyes for a moment trying to think, trying to process, trying to figure out if this was a good thing or not.

There was no doubt in his mind that he wanted to kiss Ruby. He could now accept that he'd been wanting to kiss her since he was seventeen. Now here they were again, alone, the repressed tension between them so overpowering he was finding it difficult to concentrate.

Tonight he'd danced with her, worked alongside her, walked through a quiet town with her, chatting and relaxing and having a wonderful time. Holding her in his arms and pressing his mouth to hers did seem like the next step—but Ruby wasn't just *any* woman.

Although Ruby didn't see herself as a fully fledged member of the Goldmark clan, she was indeed accepted by all of them. Lorelai wasn't his biological sister yet all of them accepted her as their own. The same could be said of Ruby. Brandon saw her as his sister. Viola saw her as the daughter she'd never had. Ruby was a special woman—not only to him but to all of them.

If he kissed her, if he allowed himself to give in to these urges surrounding them, what would happen next? What if she wasn't able to accept it just as a kiss? What if she wanted more? What if he wasn't able to *give* more? If he hurt Ruby in any way, shape or form, he knew he'd have not only Brandon to answer to but his brothers as well.

Then there was Geoffrey. Hamilton respected the other man too much. It didn't matter whether Ruby and Geoffrey were right for each other or not. The fact of the matter was that she was still dating him and as such Hamilton could not breach that union.

He'd been 'the other man' in a relationship, even though he hadn't realised it. He'd kissed another man's wife and when he'd discovered the truth, when he'd realised he'd broken the sanctity of her marriage, he'd been mortified. It hadn't mattered that Diana had told him her marriage was over. It hadn't mattered that she and her husband had been separated for the past four months. Diana had lied to him. She'd been looking for a bit of fun, an adventure, and had decided *he* was worth using. He couldn't do that to Ruby. He couldn't do that to Geoffrey. He couldn't do that to himself.

Hamilton shifted slightly and rested his forehead against hers, even though her hands at the back of his neck were angling his head so their lips could meet. He held firm, trying desperately not to think about how incredibly perfect she felt in his arms. His heart was hammering so wildly against his chest he found it difficult to grasp hold of logical thought.

'Hamilton?' she whispered, a hint of pleading in her tone.

'Just…wait a second,' he returned, confusion lacing his words. 'Ruby. What are we doing?'

'Well, *I'm* trying to kiss you. *You're* avoiding me.'

He smiled at the teasing nature of her words. 'Ruby. Be serious.'

'Are you rejecting me *again*?' There was disbelief mixed with pain in her words.

'I'm not. Ruby, I want to kiss you. More than

anything, but—' He broke off and exhaled harshly.
'We can't.'

He could feel her hands starting to go slack
around his neck, could feel the slump of her
shoulders, could feel dejection washing over her.

'You're dating Geoffrey,' he pointed out. 'I
won't kiss another man's girlfriend.'

Ruby closed her eyes and rested her head
against his chest for a moment. He was right. How
could she have forgotten Geoffrey? But she had
because the second she was close to Hamilton,
her mind could only process the way he made her
feel. So soft and feminine and cherished. 'Chivalry,' she muttered, disgusted with the word.

'Ruby, of course I want to kiss you. I'm not
rejecting you, I'm rejecting the situation. You're
an incredibly attractive woman and, yes, there
is definitely something brewing between us, but
even if Geoffrey wasn't in this equation, I can't
help feeling that even if we gave in to those feelings, right this second, come tomorrow morning,
you'd have regrets. I don't want that either.'

Ruby knew what he was saying was right. Logically, he was making complete sense but she
didn't want him to be logical. Not right now. She

wanted him to be wild and free and adventurous. She wanted him to take her away on a magic carpet ride of excitement, pleasure and epicurean delight. She edged back, his hands sliding from her hips as she released her hold on him.

'If we kissed now,' he said softly, 'you'd have trouble looking me in the eye tomorrow. You'd probably have trouble working alongside me and you don't deserve to be uncomfortable in your own home, in your own medical practice, in your own town. I'll be gone in under six months. Brandon will return and I'll head back to Tarparnii. It's all booked. Come July, I'll be back working with PMA for another six months and you'll be here, doing what you do.'

'And after that?'

He shrugged. 'I don't know. I'll see what comes up. I've been tied down to rules and regulations for far too long. At home, at medical school, at the hospital. I like moving around, experiencing new things, meeting new people and having adventures.'

He stepped back and pushed both hands through his hair with repressed frustration. 'Ruby, this is your town. I'm the interloper. We need to think logically about repercussions because *you'll* be the one dealing with them.'

'So…that's it, then? We're supposed to just ignore this crazy, ridiculous attraction burning through both of us? We're supposed to keep our distance, pretend that we're friends, that these emotions we feel—which no doubt come along so rarely in life—mean absolutely nothing?'

He could hear the pain in her voice, could see she was angry and upset, but knew it was better she was angry with him now than to have regrets later.

'It's for the best.'

Ruby shook her head and without another word turned and ran up the street. A moment later he heard her run up the five steps of her house, the front door opening and closing behind her with a hint of finality.

'It's for the best,' he whispered into the dark, deserted street.

Ruby woke after a fitful five hours of trying to sleep. Angry at herself not only for the way she'd behaved, all but begging Hamilton to kiss her, but also with the way she seemed to have lost every ounce of self-control. She kicked her legs free from the tangled bed covers and stalked to the bathroom. Turning on the water, she made sure the shower was colder than usual, hoping it would help her come to her senses if she was going to survive these next months working alongside Hamilton.

She closed her eyes and turned her face into the cool spray, grateful that he'd been the strong one last night. It hadn't been until they'd been dancing together that she'd realised she wasn't the only one trying to fight these feelings and somehow, even though it still didn't seem right, she was incredibly relieved to find she wasn't experiencing these weird sensations alone.

The fact that Hamilton *had* wanted to kiss her was almost a relief. At least she wouldn't be burdened with the sensations that he'd rejected her advances yet again. Still, accepting that he was as attracted to her as she was to him would only make it harder to fight. She shook her head, the water cascading down her neck. She could recall with far too much clarity exactly what it had felt like to touch the firm contours of his chest, the broadness of his shoulders, the sensation of his breath mingling with hers, their lips so incredibly close yet so far apart.

'What's wrong with you? Why are you attracted to *him*?' Ruby reached for the shampoo and began washing her hair with extra vigour, as though she could wash her attraction for Hamilton right out of her hair. Life would have been so much easier if she'd been able to fall in love with Geoffrey. He was a good, honest, hard-working man who doted on her. He loved Lewisville as much as she did and wanted only the best for the townsfolk. The problem was, she saw Geoffrey as nothing but a friend. Sighing, she also realised it was unfair to string him along, allowing him to hope that one day she'd be ready to settle down. If last night's escapades with Hamilton had shown her anything, it was that there wasn't that dynamic, powerful chemistry between herself and the Lewisville police officer.

Even her own parents' marriage hadn't been one filled with honour, love and trust. They'd both been so desperate to find their treasure, both adamant that the next big score would solve all their problems, pay all their debts, get them out of the hole they'd dug for themselves.

To go from that sort of family life to one of pure love between Viola and Bill Goldmark had been like all her Christmases coming true. They'd nurtured her, cared for her and put her through school, encouraging her to persevere when she'd been teased for being further behind in her studies than other kids her age. She'd been given a big brother in Brandon and a town filled with people willing to help. Her cup had been filled with blessings and it had overflowed.

It was why she felt honour bound to stay in Lewisville, to provide medical support for the community that had taken her in and loved her. It was why she knew she needed to talk to Geoffrey today, to be honest, to let him know that there could never be anything between them but friendship. It was why she knew she must keep her distance from Hamilton—a man who would never stay in one place, always going where the next adventure took him. Her parents had been like that, their nomadic existence often causing them more problems than anything else. She couldn't live a life like that. Not again.

Sighing, Ruby finished her shower, feeling a little calmer than when she'd woken. After dressing and drying her hair, twisting it up into a loose, messy bun, she headed out to the kitchen, hoping she hadn't woken Vi. The hope was in vain as Viola was standing at the stove, cooking up some bacon and eggs. Toast popped and the coffee was almost finished.

'Morning, Vi,' she said. Viola jumped almost half a mile and Ruby smiled. 'Sorry.' She kissed Vi's cheek. 'Didn't mean to startle you.'

'Oh, I was hoping you'd sleep in this morning.'

Ruby shrugged and snagged a piece of bacon from the frying pan. Viola swatted at her hand with the spatula but missed. 'Too much to get done.' Ruby kissed Vi's cheek again, grinning.

'I didn't hear you come in last night.'

'It was fairly late. About two o'clock this morning.' Ruby continued eating her bacon as she opened the fridge and retrieved the orange juice, pouring herself a glass.

'How's Marissa? Is she on the mend?'

'Mrs M. was stable when we left,' she reported. 'I haven't had the chance to ring the hospital yet this morning.'

'I have,' a deep voice said from behind her, and

she turned, coming face to face with Hamilton as he walked in the front door. Her body froze. 'She's doing wonderfully. ECG readings are in the normal range. They've transferred her to a ward and she was sitting up having a cup of tea when I spoke to her.' He looked past Ruby as he walked into the kitchen and kissed Viola's cheek. 'Mmm. Breakfast smells good.'

'I'm glad you were able to make it,' Viola said, then addressed her comment to Ruby. 'I bumped into Hamilton when I went out for my walk this morning.'

Hamilton met Ruby's gaze. 'I couldn't sleep,' he ventured. 'Probably too much excitement last night.' He raised an eyebrow in a teasing manner and she glared at him. She had hoped he wouldn't refer, mention or allude to what had transpired between them. It seemed she was wrong. The fiend.

'Yes, bush dances do cause quite a stir,' Viola agreed, her back to them, as she started to dish up a plateful of food, unaware of the undercurrents passing between Ruby and Hamilton. 'But I thought you would have been used to the social side of things, Ham. I thought all you young people living in big cities enjoyed all the night life.'

An incredibly sexy smile slowly spread over his lips as he continued to hold Ruby's gaze. 'We don't have nearly as much excitement in the city as you do here in the Outback. Nothing that *really* gets the heart pumping.' His words were pointed and filled with double entendres. 'It's... very different here but still incredibly enjoyable.'

Ruby rolled her eyes at him, shaking her head against his teasing. She turned away and drank the rest of her orange juice, her appetite disappearing due to the fluttering of butterflies in her stomach. With one powerful smile he'd managed to make her knees weaken, her heart pound faster and her anxiety rise. She'd been under the assumption that as he *hadn't* followed through on the desire to kiss her last night that he would also stop teasing and flirting with her. Obviously she'd been wrong. 'I'm going to the clinic.' Her tone was firm as she reached for her spare hat near the door.

'But, Ruby,' Viola protested, turning to face Ruby, holding out a plate of food, 'what about breakfast?'

'Sorry, Vi.' She glared pointedly at Hamilton. 'Lost my appetite.' With that, she walked out the door.

Hamilton wasn't sure what type of reception he was going to receive from Ruby the next time they met but discovered it was one of polite professionalism. He hadn't meant to tease her when Viola had invited him for breakfast but he simply hadn't been able to resist. When he'd walked into the house and seen her standing there dressed in a pair of black three-quarter pants and a russet-red top that seemed to highlight her perfectly sculpted face, her vibrant green eyes and dark hair loosely knotted on top of her head, tendrils hanging down…he'd had to swallow twice before he'd been able to speak.

The woman literally took his breath away and where he'd hoped this burning attraction he felt for her would settle down the longer he was in Lewisville, every time he saw her the reaction was the same. That initial breathlessness, that tightening in his gut, that overpowering need to have her pressed firmly against his body, his mouth on hers giving them the satisfaction they continued to deny.

As he'd been unable to sleep, thoughts of Ruby infiltrating his dreams far too deeply, Hamilton had decided to go for a walk and it had been in the middle of the street that he'd bumped into his cousin.

'You're up early,' Viola had said. 'I'm just on my way to Filmore's farm to get some fresh eggs for breakfast.'

'You don't drive?'

'What? And miss being able to walk in the coolest part of the day? Perish the thought.'

'Would you like some company?' he'd offered.

Viola had smiled brightly. 'I'd love some.'

So the two of them had headed to Mr Filmore's farm and collected the eggs, Viola waving to her friend, saying, 'Put them on my account,' as they headed back into town. 'You should be wearing your hat,' Viola had chastised, and then quickly remembered. 'That's right. I have it at my place. Why don't you drop around for breakfast and pick it up?'

Hamilton had hesitated, not sure whether it would be a good idea to see Ruby so soon after what had happened—or hadn't happened—between them last night. 'Uh…I can pick it up later. No drama.'

'No drama! Out here not wearing a hat, especially in the middle of the day, is most definitely a drama, Hamilton Goldmark. No, you'll stop by for breakfast and you can pick up your hat then.'

Hamilton had frowned. 'I'll stop by but I won't stay for breakfast. I wouldn't want to intrude.'

'You mean you wouldn't want to bump into Ruby, eh?'

Hamilton had been so surprised by her words that he'd stopped short. 'What?'

Viola had laughed. 'Do you think I'm blind as well as stupid?'

'I don't think you're either.'

'Good. Then you won't mind me saying that it's about time someone swept Ruby off her feet.' Viola had linked her free arm through Hamilton's as they'd started walking again. 'I'm glad it's you.'

'What? Wait, Viola, I—'

'I saw the two of you last night at the dance. There's chemistry between you. Just like there was between me and my Bill…and your mum and dad had it, too.'

Hamilton raised his eyebrows. 'You're not angry?'

'Angry? Why would I be angry? I think it's fantastic!'

'You do?' Hamilton was stunned.

'Ruby needs someone who's going to give her a run for her money, who isn't going to do whatever she says, like poor Geoffrey.'

'You don't like Geoffrey?'

'Oh, I do. I love Geoffrey and I have done ever since he was a teenager, but I also know he's not right for Ruby. He can't even see that Joan's all but smitten with him.'

'Ah, yes, Joan. I thought as much.'

'Yes. It's a real little love mix-up but as soon as Ruby lets Geoffrey down, I'm sure he'll start taking notice of Joan.'

'Ruby's going to break up with Geoffrey?' Hamilton was secretly delighted at this news but tried to keep his tone neutral.

'If I know my Ruby, she'll be doing it soon. She'd never lead anyone on, especially not Geoffrey. She cares about him a lot but she doesn't love him.'

'So…you don't have a problem if Ruby…er… should Ruby and…er, I…um… Not that I'm saying we would because…well…things are complicated but…*if*…we…' He stopped trying to talk and shook his head, unable to believe how ridiculous he sounded.

Viola laughed again as Hamilton tripped over his words. 'I take it you'll be coming for breakfast, then?'

Hamilton looked into her wise eyes and joined in with her laughter. 'I believe I am.'

And so he'd gone for breakfast only to be met with a storming Ruby, annoyed with him for teasing her, but he'd been unable to stop.

Now, as they continued on throughout the day, keeping their distance from each other, Hamilton started to wonder whether Viola had imagined things. When Geoffrey stopped by just after lunch, Ruby greeted him with a kiss that clearly answered the question as to whether she'd ended things with the police officer. Hamilton looked away, not wanting to watch them. It was then his gaze had fallen on Joan, who had looked as though her heart was breaking at the sight before her.

Joan *did* carry a torch for Geoffrey. It was clearly written all over her face, so if Viola had been right about that, surely she was right about Ruby ending her romantic relationship. If she did, what would that mean for the two of them? Was he willing to take a chance with Ruby and put his heart out there again? When Diana had pulverised his heart, it had taken him quite some time to recover, but with Ruby…it had the potential to be far worse.

By the end of his second week in Lewisville, nothing had changed between Ruby and himself. Viola had issued him with several dinner invitations but for Ruby's sake he'd decided to decline. Brandon had called, asking how he was settling into life in an Outback town and Hamilton had found himself responding with evasive answers. Even just talking to Brandon made him feel guilty as every night Hamilton still found himself dreaming about Ruby.

He'd heard through the rampant gossiping that went on in the waiting room that Ruby had indeed ended her relationship with Geoffrey.

'He's heartbroken,' one woman had said.

'I saw him in the pub the other night, drinking a beer—full strength,' the other had replied, and both had gasped at this news. Hamilton, however, hadn't noticed anything out of the ordinary where Geoffrey was concerned. The two men had become quite good friends and Geoffrey hadn't appeared to be pining for Ruby at all. Along with Parker and some of the other men in town, he and Geoffrey had decided to build Brandon's planned garage. It would not only be a surprise for his cousin but also provided much-needed shelter for Hamilton's sports car.

'Time for another orange juice?' Hamilton said later that night as he and Geoffrey had drinks at the pub.

Geoffrey shook his head and stood. 'Sorry, mate, but I've been invited out for dinner tonight.'

'Where? If it's with Mrs Mandocicelli, tell her to go easy on the cholesterol. She's back to full health but we don't want another nasty episode.'

Geoffrey laughed, then looked down at his feet, a hint of shyness creeping into his demeanour. 'It's not Mrs M.'s. Actually, I'm headed over to Joan's house.'

'Joan's!' Hamilton grinned. Good for Joan, he thought. 'Well, well, well.'

'Yes.' Geoffrey's smile grew wider. 'She's going to cook me dinner.'

Hamilton slapped his friend on the shoulder. 'I like a man who doesn't let the grass grow under his feet. Off you go. You don't want to keep her waiting.'

Geoffrey nodded and had taken two steps away before turning back to look at him. 'Hey, Ham?'

'Yeah?' Hamilton had just ordered another lemonade. He was on call tonight, he and Ruby taking it in turns, so no alcohol for him.

'About Ruby.'

Hamilton's smile slipped from his face and he felt a sense of impending doom settle over him. As though by unspoken mutual consent, the topic of Ruby had been taboo between them...until now. 'Yeah?'

'It's chemistry, mate. You can't fight it.' With a brief nod Geoffrey turned and left the pub, leaving Hamilton to wonder whether the cop had just given him his blessing.

It was a thought he pondered as he made his way back to the unit. He couldn't stop thinking about Ruby. Viola and now Geoffrey didn't seem to mind if he wanted to date Ruby. The woman in question, however, wasn't even speaking to him, let alone wanting to pursue a romantic connection. Why would she? He'd made it clear he wasn't planning to stay in Lewisville come the end of his contract. He'd be off, on his way to Tarparnii, leaving her behind.

'Unless she came with you,' he murmured, hope rising for a split second, then he shook his head. No. It was better this way. They'd be polite and indifferent colleagues, seeing each other now and then at the odd family get-together. This mounting attraction he didn't seem able to shake would dissipate as soon as he left Lewisville. It had to because no woman had ever meant this much to him before—not even Diana—and Ruby was far too important for him to trifle with her emotions.

Hamilton reached for the remote control, already knowing there wouldn't be anything on the television but still going through the motions. Wasn't that what life was about? Going through the motions until you found that one elusive person who brought you so much joy, your world changed for ever? That's the way it seemed to have happened for his brothers. Would it be like that for him? Was Ruby that elusive person? Had he already found her?

A sharp knock at his door made him spring to his feet. 'Hamilton?'

'Ruby?' He instantly switched off the television, his heart starting to thump wildly as he stalked impatiently to the door. Ruby was here!

'There's an emergency,' she said as he opened the door. Hamilton's gaze flicked over her, taking in her concerned eyes and worried frown, and he knew he'd do whatever she needed if it meant her brow would clear and her eyes could once again be filled with happiness. The realisation momentarily stunned him.

'It's Mr Eddington. His wife stopped me on my way home and I went to take a look. I'm fairly certain it's appendicitis but I want a second opinion.' Her words tumbled over each other as she headed back towards the clinic.

'I'm sure your diagnosis is accurate. Where is he?'

'He's still at home but I was going to call Joan and Geoffrey and get them to organise a stretcher in case we need to move him to the clinic if we have to operate.'

'Good thinking.' Hamilton followed her to the back door of the clinic. 'But let's not worry Joan and Geoffrey just yet,' he said thinking of the date they were hopefully enjoying. 'I'm sure Ned Finnegan can give me a hand with the stretcher as he lives next door to the Eddingtons.' Hamilton went to a long cupboard and pulled out the emergency stretcher. 'I think it's best if we get Albert back here, stat. You get everything ready in the emergency room. If it's required, are you able to give an anaesthetic?'

'Yes.'

'Good. Get the room set up and I'll see to his transfer.'

'Do you want me to ring for the chopper?'

'The chopper or the RFDS, whichever is easiest. Even if we can operate and stabilise Albert, he'll still require hospitalisation but the transfer won't be urgent.'

'OK.' Ruby sighed as Hamilton headed for the door. 'I'm really glad you're here,' she said, and he turned and smiled at her over his shoulder, pleased to note her brow was no longer furrowed and her eyes were filled with hope. The sight warmed his heart.

By the time Hamilton and Ned carried Mr Eddington into the clinic a little later, Ruby was as ready as she could be. She could also hear Ned's wife, May, and Mrs Eddington out in the waiting room. She wanted to go to them, to reassure them that everything would be all right, that because Hamilton was here, Mr Eddington would be fine—but she had a job to do. It wasn't often she had to give an anaesthetic and thankfully it would only be a minor surgical procedure, but keeping her thoughts focused on the job at hand was of paramount importance, especially as she'd never operated alongside Hamilton before.

Once Mr Eddington was settled on the operating table, Ned and May Finnegan out in the waiting room keeping Mrs Eddington company, Hamilton headed to the scrub sink, while Ruby spoke to Albert as she wound the blood-pressure cuff around one of his arms and prepared to insert a drip into the other.

'How are we doing?' Hamilton asked, glancing over at her.

'Good,' she returned, then continued to speak

softly to Albert, explaining how she'd be administering the anaesthetic.

Once Hamilton had finished scrubbing, he pulled on a sterile gown and some surgical gloves. 'Ready?'

'Yes.' She watched as he looked at the equipment she'd prepared, his eyes widening with delight.

'You have a laparoscope? Brilliant!'

She smiled. 'All the money raised from last year's bush dances went into purchasing it but until now we haven't had to use it.'

'Brandon hasn't had a turn?'

Ruby shook her head. 'And he'll no doubt be quite jealous you got to go first.'

'Well,' Hamilton said, as he sterilised and draped Mr Eddington's abdomen, 'it can't be helped. Mr Eddington here needs me to operate.' He looked up at the ceiling. 'Sorry, cuz,' he said to the absent Brandon.

Ruby's smile increased at his antics and she was pleased that he seemed more than familiar with the equipment. 'Are you ready to proceed?' she asked.

He nodded. 'With this shiny new toy? Oh, yes.

I've been so used to doing this type of surgery the old-fashioned way via laparotomy, especially in Tarparnii, but it's all starting to come back to me now.'

'Pleased to hear it.'

'If you don't mind,' he said once he was ready, 'I'll talk my way through the entire procedure. That way, we both know what I'm doing and you can assist me when necessary,' he said, looking at the monitor, which would show him exactly what he'd be seeing once he had the laparoscope inserted into Albert's abdomen.

As it turned out, Albert Eddington's appendix was incredibly close to perforating and thankfully Hamilton, with Ruby's assistance, was able to remove it before things turned critical. Working together, Ruby realised just what a great team she and Hamilton made.

'Just as well we made the decision to operate,' he remarked as he put sticking plasters over the two small incisions he'd made. Ruby reversed the anaesthetic and Mr Eddington slowly came round.

'Mr Eddington?' she called. 'Can you hear me?

Albert?' At the sound of the man's incoherent words, both of them smiled.

'Good. He's coming round. I'll go speak to his wife and give her the good news.' With that, Hamilton degowned and headed out of the small room, pleased to see the RFDS pilot in the waiting room as well. Once both he and Ruby were satisfied with Albert's condition, the RFDS nursing staff were more than capable of supervising the transfer to Broken Hill, Mrs Eddington accompanying her husband on the flight.

'Thanks for all your help tonight,' Hamilton said to Ned and May. 'That's what I love about Lewisville. You really rally around and take care of your own.'

Ned puffed out his chest, as proud as punch, and was about to start on one of his long speeches about just how much he and his wife did for the town when Ruby stepped forward and opened the front door to the clinic.

'Thanks again so much,' she said. 'Hamilton and I need to clean the emergency room now, ensuring it's as ready as can be—just in case.'

'Of course,' Ned returned. 'Just in case.' And within another moment Ruby and Hamilton were waving goodbye to the Finnegans and closing the clinic door, bolting it from the inside. It wasn't until she turned to face a smiling Hamilton that she realised she was once more alone with him. Her breath caught in her throat.

Self-consciousness started to wind itself around her and after a brief glance at his smiling face, she quickly headed to the emergency room. The sooner they were able to clean it and go their separate ways, the better.

Did he know she'd broken up with Geoffrey? She hadn't said anything but of course he would know. The whole town knew because everyone knew everything. She shook her head as she began clearing equipment away, either disposing of it or getting it ready for sterilisation. Now that she was single again, would it change the powerful and overwhelming attraction that still existed so vibrantly between them?

When Hamilton entered the room, Ruby decided it was best to keep up a steady stream of chatter. 'You really know your way around a laparoscope,' she remarked, and closed her eyes for a second, unable to believe how incredibly lame that had sounded.

'It was a fun toy to play with.'

'Well, I'm sure Albert appreciates your desire to try it out. I'm also glad you were trained. If you hadn't been here…' She let her words trail off. 'Still, I guess that's why Brandon thought to ask you to fill in, because he knew you held the qualifications necessary to perform such surgery.'

'You could learn, too,' he offered.

'What do you mean?'

'Do more qualifications. The town is holding bush dance after bush dance, raising funds so this clinic can procure such amazing equipment. It's kind of a shame you don't get to play with it.'

'I'll play with the digital X-ray machine when it arrives,' she replied, a hint of annoyance in her tone.

'All I'm saying is that you don't have to settle for not learning new techniques. Even if you have to go to Sydney for the odd training course, the possibilities aren't out of your reach. Plus, in the end, it'll benefit the people of the town you love so much.'

When she didn't reply, he continued. 'Do you ever think you might be stuck in a rut here?'

'You're saying I should leave? Go and have adventures, like you do?'

'I'm saying you're a brilliant, talented and intelligent woman, Ruby. Why limit yourself? I'm not suggesting you leave Lewisville permanently. It's your home, just as Oodnaminaby is my home, but that doesn't mean you shouldn't be able to pursue other areas that interest you. I saw the way you were watching the operation, watching it as though *you* wanted to learn how to do that.'

Ruby's eyes widened. How had he seen that? It was true. She had been thinking that and she knew it was all possible, that everything he was saying was correct, but still…something was holding her back.

'Where are Joan and Geoffrey?' she asked, wanting to change the subject. 'I thought they would have heard what was happening and come running.'

'Well…actually, they're having dinner.'

'I know. Joan said she'd invited him round. So?'

'As in a dinner *date*,' Hamilton added, and then watched as dawning realisation crossed Ruby's face.

'Oh. *Oh!*' She blinked once. 'Joan?'

He nodded.

'And Geoffrey?'

'Does it bother you? You and Geoffrey only broke up, what, about a week or so ago?'

Ruby shook her head. 'It doesn't bother me. I just had no idea Joan had feelings for him.'

'According to Viola, she's been harbouring them for some time.'

'Vi told you? Why didn't she tell me?' Ruby felt left out, as though everyone knew what was going on except her.

'Probably because you were dating Geoffrey and she didn't want to cause a conflict of interest.'

'But, still, she should have said something, not tell everyone else.' Ruby pointed to Hamilton as she spoke.

'I'm not *everyone else*. I'm her cousin.' Hamilton took off his gloves and put them in the bin with the rest of the rubbish, the room now back to its proper sterile level. Both of them headed to the door, Hamilton taking out his keys to lock the room behind them.

'You know what I mean.' Ruby sighed, her

shoulders slumping, her tone dejected. 'I just feel so…disjointed.'

'Ruby.' Hamilton reached out a hand towards her but she quickly stepped away.

'No, don't… I just can't… If you touch me, I'll…' She stopped and sighed again. 'I don't know. I'm so confused.'

'If it helps, you're not the only one.'

Ruby looked at him, her eyes filled with repressed desire and a whole lot of pain, which he was sure was reflected in his own eyes. 'It's better this way, right? You and me? Apart?'

He nodded. 'I think so.'

She pursed her lips together and nodded, as though she was desperately trying to hold onto the tears that were threatening to spill over. Then with a sob she turned and ran out the back door of the clinic.

Hamilton's throat choked over as he watched her go, the sound of her anguish filling not only the air around him but pulsing through his entire body. He took two steps to follow her then stopped, clenching his fists at his sides.

He shook his head. 'It can't be right. It just can't be.'

CHAPTER NINE

IN THE middle of Hamilton's third week in Lewisville, Ruby came into his consulting office, standing close to the doorway and refusing his offer of a chair.

'I can't stay. My next patient has just arrived.'

'Last one for the day?' he asked.

'Yes. Anyway, I've been meaning to tell you that we'll be heading out of town for the next three days.' Since they'd almost kissed, she'd managed to control her thoughts during the day but the nights were a completely different story. Images, dreams, visions. Need, want, desire. They'd all blended together to give her such powerful experiences she'd often woken up with Hamilton's name on her lips.

'House calls.' Hamilton nodded.

Ruby frowned. 'You know?'

'I noticed there were no patients scheduled for the rest of the week so I asked Joan about it. She told me how she holds the fort, providing first aid where necessary, and that you and I go off to surrounding properties, holding clinics and doing check-ups at various places.'

'That's right.'

'Sounds like an adventure.' He rubbed his hands together with glee.

'It's not an adventure, Hamilton. It's work.' There was a hint of desperation to her tone. 'Work and only work.'

'Of course.' A polite smile touched his mouth. 'Shall we take my car or yours?'

Ruby closed her eyes for a moment, visions of driving around in the spacious Outback in Hamilton's sports car, the roof down, just the two of them out in the sunshine, her hair blowing in the wind, came to mind. It was the classic romantic picture advertisers would use to sell the car in the first place. No. She didn't want any part of any sort of romantic scenario and especially not with Hamilton.

'I was joking,' he replied when she didn't speak. Ruby's eyes snapped open and she glared at him.

'Don't joke with me, Hamilton.' Her tone was

low but pointed. 'We're colleagues. That's all. Nothing more. Understood?'

Hamilton inclined his head just a fraction, unable to believe just how tightly she was wound. This whole attraction thing flaring between them was really starting to bother her. Of course it bothered him too but he didn't want to make things worse for Ruby than they already were. He was as much to blame as she was for the situation they found themselves in.

'I need to show you the ropes of what to do on house calls,' she continued. 'Next time you'll be heading out with Joan instead.'

'Ruby, listen. I'm sorry abo—'

She held up a hand to stop him. 'I don't want to hear what you're sorry about. I don't care. You're my colleague. You've proven yourself to be excellent at the job, the patients all think you're great, and that's all that really matters.'

With that, she turned and stalked from his consulting room, leaving Hamilton scratching his head in confusion.

Hamilton flicked through the radio stations, shaking his head when all he received was static.

'Now, that's how you know you really are out in the middle of nowhere. There's no radio reception.' He shook his head and glanced across at Ruby, who was concentrating on her driving.

'So…is there somewhere I can plug in my MP3 player?'

Ruby glanced across at him but as she was wearing sunglasses, he couldn't see her eyes. He guessed she was giving him some sort of glare. She returned her gaze to the road but didn't say a word.

'I'll take that as a no. OK, well, if there's no music, you leave me no option but to sing you a song.' He cleared his throat and dragged in a breath. *'Lah!'* He released a high-pitched note, imitating an opera singer. Ruby turned her head sharply but he could see the corners of her mouth starting to twitch in an upwards direction. Good. They'd been in the car for over half an hour now and he'd had barely a word out of her. There was no way he was going to endure three full days of silence from her, especially when he was desperate to try and find an even footing for the two of them to traverse for the remainder of his time in Lewisville.

He shook his head and cleared his throat again, thumping his chest with his fist. 'Hang on. Let me try that again.' This time he released a smooth baritone note. 'Much better.'

She still didn't talk but nodded as she returned her attention to the long, straight, flat road before them. They'd started off quite early so they weren't driving during the heat of the day. The sun was just starting to rise and it was at this time of day, as well as dusk, that was worst for kangaroos to be near the roads.

'Any requests?' he asked, but only received a nonchalant shrug of her shoulders as a reply. 'All right. Be it on your own head.' And with that he began to sing a country song the band had played at the bush dance a few weeks ago. 'Join in if you know the words,' he added between verses. No reply. Hamilton kept on singing, knowing she had to give in and talk to him at some point. They had a three-hour drive to get to their first stop for the day, then, after doing a morning clinic at the Moffat homestead, they would jump back in the car to drive another four hours to the Davis homestead, where they'd set up in preparation for tomorrow's clinic. He'd been warned it was a gruelling schedule.

At the end of the song he pretended there was an enormous round of applause. 'Thank you, thank you.' He blew kisses to the imaginary audience and fanned his face as though overcome with emotion. 'Oh, you're *too* kind.'

Ruby finally laughed and shook her head. 'You're impossible!' Her words were filled with a mixture of annoyance and humour.

'Impossible to ignore?'

'Apparently.'

'Ah, but at least you're talking to me now.'

Ruby sighed. 'Things are just…confusing.'

'I know but can't we forget what almost happened or what didn't almost happen and go back to being friends?'

'I don't know.'

'Well, let's at least call a truce while we're away. What do you think about that?'

Ruby thought for a moment. 'It would be silly to keep ignoring you, especially when we're forced to spend so much time together.'

'Exactly.' Relieved he'd managed to ingratiate

himself back into her good books, he cleared his throat. 'Now…shall we sing a duet together?'

'I have some CDs in the glove box.'

'What? And ruin my concert? Perish the thought.'

Ruby giggled as he overacted his words and when he started to sing another song, this time she joined in, their voices blending perfectly.

When they arrived at the Moffat homestead, with Hamilton more than happy to jump out every now and then to open the large gates for them to drive through, it was almost nine o'clock in the morning. Already around the large homestead there were quite a few cars, people getting out to greet and chat with each other. In addition to the homestead, there were also three other smaller cottages and Ruby had explained they were for the families of the foreman and overseers of the two-thousand-acre property.

'What time is the clinic due to start?' Hamilton asked with an impending sense of doom as he looked around.

'We have an hour to set up but you have to remember, not only do clinics provide medical care, it's also another social event. Some of these people live in such remote areas that they don't see anyone outside their own family and work-force for weeks and sometimes months on end,' she explained as she pulled her four-wheel-drive into a space near the front steps, ensuring eas-ier access for carrying their equipment inside. 'It's why Lewisville tries to have regular social events, even though most of them are fundrais-ers. That way, Outback life doesn't feel so lonely or isolated.'

'When is the next big shindig?' Hamilton asked, unbuckling his seat belt and opening his door, the heat of the morning hitting him with full force as he climbed from the air-conditioned vehicle. Not only did the heat hit him but the flies as well. He swatted them away in what was be-coming an ingrained habit.

'St Valentine's Day,' Ruby replied as she ex-ited and walked round to the rear of the vehicle.

'A Valentine's Day bush dance for Ruby Valentine?'

Ruby shook her head. 'Not a bush dance. It's an all-out, dressed-to-the-nines, proper party. The girls wear their shiniest dresses and the guys have to wear suits.'

'Suits? In this heat?'

'If you don't wear your suit, you can't dance with the pretty girls.'

Hamilton picked up a large crate from the back of her four-wheel-drive but stopped and met her gaze. 'Do you already have your dress?'

Ruby nodded slowly, her eyes sparkling, her mouth curved into an alluring smile. She leaned forward, whispering, 'It's a knockout. It's dark and sleek and very sexy.' She drawled the last two words and all sorts of images of Ruby walking towards him in a dark, sleek and very sexy dress filled his mind.

Hamilton's gaze dipped to her mouth, unable to believe how with just a few whispered words she'd managed to release the control button on his hormones that he'd been working so hard to keep locked and under control. He swallowed over his suddenly dry throat as her slow and pointed words swirled around him. He was captivated by her.

'You…will…*love*…' her tongue touched her lips and he almost gasped with the implied innuendo '…it.'

Hamilton swallowed compulsively, his gaze

drawn to her mouth, watching as her lips curved into a slow and alluring smile. He looked up into her sparkling green eyes, realising that she'd purposely set him on fire. He eased back, straightening his shoulders. 'Hey. That's unfair,' he murmured, his tone equally as soft and as intimate as hers. 'We said we'd be friends. No flirting allowed.'

Ruby raised an eyebrow, her lips curving in that way that caused his gut to tighten. 'I remember no such rule.' With that, she hefted a box into her arms and headed up the steps into the homestead.

Hamilton watched her go, his gaze riveted to the sway of her sexy body, desperate to get his breathing back under control as well as the rest of his hormones. Even though they'd been doing their best to steer clear of each other during the past few weeks, he had to wonder whether he was going to be able to survive the next few days, especially if she was going to flirt with him!

They set up and started clinic fairly close to time, both of them seeing a steady stream of patients for the next three hours. At one o'clock, they stopped and headed out to the rear veranda, where Susie Moffat and a number of the other women who had brought their children to the clinic had provided enough food to feed everyone there. Hamilton smiled and joined in, enjoying himself immensely.

'You've adjusted quickly,' Ruby commented when she came and sat down next to him, both of them looking out to the back yard where there seemed to be a plethora of children, all doused in sunscreen and wearing hats, playing and laughing and running around enjoying themselves.

'To what?' Hamilton sipped his long, cool iced tea.

'The strange set-up, the clinics, the people.'

Hamilton shrugged. 'It's not so different from how we work in Tarparnii. The only real difference is they don't have rambling big houses such as this one. We use large tents. Other than that, I'm more than used to carting all necessary medical equipment from place to place and seeing patient after patient.'

'Really?' Ruby thoughtfully processed his words. 'I guess I hadn't considered it much before.'

'There is one other difference between here and Tarparnii.'

'What's that?'

'The number of patients.'

Ruby agreed. 'This is a fairly large one. People have come from all around the district, asking for help with every tiny ailment.'

Hamilton chuckled. 'You misunderstand me. In Tarparnii, we'd see an average of one hundred people per clinic day. So far in the last three hours I've seen about twenty. Then again,' he continued when Ruby gaped at him, 'we usually have about six or seven of us running the clinics so it helps when you're dealing with such large volumes of patients.'

'One hundred? Wow!' She shook her head slowly. 'It sounds powerful and impressive and scary all at the same time.'

Hamilton laughed again and finished his drink. 'And adventurous.' He winked. 'You should volunteer with PMA some time. I think you'd love it.' He paused and tried to keep his tone calm. 'Or, if you wanted, you could come over with me when I've finished my contract here. Give Brandon a taste of what it's like being left to hold the fort on your own with a locum who doesn't know the ropes.'

'You've actually been quite easy on me...er... to work with, I mean,' she quickly clarified, trying not to blush at her slip of the tongue.

Hamilton nodded. 'Well, thank you, Ruby, but as I've said, after working in Tarparnii as well as with the Nocturnal Outreach Welfare in Canberra, I've become used to adaptive medicine. In Tarparnii we don't have even half the equipment you have in Lewisville. It's raw, it's tough, but, by gum, it's rewarding.'

'By gum?' she teased, smiling at his expression.

'Yep. By gum,' he repeated. 'You learn cool words like that when you travel.' He stood and straightened his shoulders, allowing Ruby's soft chuckles to wash over him. She had such a pretty laugh. He'd do anything to hear it more often. He also had to admit that out here, away from the township of Lewisville, she even seemed a bit more...relaxed. It wasn't that she was uptight but almost as though when she was in town there was an added pressure weighing heavily on her shoulders. He knew she was conscious of always doing her best, of never letting people down. Out here, though, things were a bit more relaxed. He liked the look of a stressless Ruby.

'You're very pretty,' he said, the words escaping before he could stop them.

'Hey, now.' She held up one hand to stop him. 'No flirting, remember.'

Hamilton shrugged. 'I remember no such rule,' he stated, repeating her earlier words. That caused Ruby to smile and shake her head as she stood and pointed to the patients who were starting to finish up their meals.

'I guess we'd better get back to it.'

'Before something…crazy happens between us?' he asked softly.

Ruby looked into his eyes, tingles of excited awareness zinging through her. 'Exactly.' And pulling superhuman strength from goodness knew where, she turned and headed towards the front rooms of the homestead that had been set aside for them to use as consulting rooms.

Hamilton watched her go, breathing out slowly in an effort to try and control the urges he was desperately trying to fight.

The Moffats had even provided small camp

beds to make it easier for the doctors to examine their patients. Hamilton saw several people with skin allergies, two people who had vision problems and a whole company of men from one property who were required to have inoculations or else the boss would sack them. A few people had more serious injuries that required follow-up treatment and so he made appointments for them to come to Lewisville. Ruby saw most of the female patients. Many of the women were pregnant, requiring a general check-up to ensure all was right with mother and child. Ruby had packed the foetal heart-rate monitor specifically for the purpose of not only checking the baby's heart rate for herself but also to allow the expectant mothers to hear it, too.

By four o'clock, the patients were dwindling, as many people needed to leave to complete the one- or two-hour drive back to their own homes and properties.

'I think the vastness here is the biggest difference from Tarparnii,' Hamilton commented to Ruby as they packed up their equipment.

'Is it a big country?' she asked, really interested in what he was saying. Hamilton needed no prompting to talk about the place he considered his second home. He told her about his friends and described the lush greenness of the villages, the way everyone pulled together to help each other out. 'The sense of community is the same as it is in Lewisville.'

'I like that the most,' she said as they put the last crate into the car. 'I like feeling a part of everything, of helping and supporting and working towards a common goal.' The wind had started to pick up and a piece of her long brown hair blew across her cheek.

'That's admirable,' he told her, instinctively reaching out to tuck the strand behind her ear. As soon as he'd done it, he realised it had been the wrong thing to do, especially with the way her soft, smooth skin had felt beneath his fingertips. Ruby gasped at the touch and instantly licked her dry lips as though she were getting ready for something more than a simple brush of his fingers against her skin.

'Sorry,' he murmured, unable to look away from her vibrant green eyes.

'It's OK,' she returned, her voice trembling a little as she spoke.

'No, it's not, because every time I touch you, I just want to touch you even more.' He shook his head and shoved his hands into the pockets of his denim jeans. 'I've been trying to keep my distance, Ruby, honestly I have.'

'I know.' She inched a little closer, her heart pounding wildly against her chest. 'What do we do?'

He shook his head. 'Fight it?'

'You don't sound too sure.'

'I'm not.' He exhaled slowly.

Ruby closed her eyes for a moment then nodded, glancing at him once more before turning away, amazed at how she could walk on legs that felt like jelly. 'We'd better be on our way. We have a good four hours' drive ahead of us and we definitely want to get to the Davis homestead before the sun sets.' She headed up the front steps into the house, feeling rather than knowing Hamilton was right behind her.

'Just as well it's daylight saving,' he ventured, but received no further comment.

After they'd offered their thanks, accepting a 'stay awake' package from Susie, which contained mini-cakes, biscuits and a refilled Thermos of coffee, they said their goodbyes to the Moffats and headed to the car.

'I'll take the first shift,' Hamilton said. 'You can navigate or have a rest if you like. Then we can switch.'

'Sure.' The fact that she hadn't argued with him made him wonder if she was going to slip back into silence mode where all he would manage to pull from her were monosyllables, *if* he was lucky. She opened the glove compartment and found a CD, slipping it into the player, the soothing sounds of her favourite band filling the air. Hamilton wasn't sure whether she'd put it on to help them both stay awake or whether it was so they didn't have to talk. However, after the first hour both of them seemed more relaxed, singing along to the songs and laughing when they got the words wrong. Four hours later, when they arrived at the Davis homestead, they were tired but happy.

'That was a great trip,' she remarked after they'd unloaded the car. Their hosts for the night were very welcoming but after showing Hamilton and Ruby to their rooms left them alone, citing the need to be up early in the morning.

'There's the smell of rain in the air,' Russ Davis remarked. 'Bad rain. I wanna get my stock to higher ground.'

'Do you think it's going to rain tomorrow?' Ruby asked, instantly concerned. Experienced property owners like Russ knew the weather patterns better than any meteorologist.

'Nah. Not until Friday, but it's coming. I can feel it in me bones.' With a nod of his head Russ went to bed, waving his hand towards the kitchen. 'Help yourselves to whatever you want.'

When he'd gone, Hamilton turned to look at Ruby. 'How are you feeling? Tired?'

'Actually, no. I'm pretty wired.' She laughed as they headed into the kitchen of the quiet homestead. She noticed as they walked that Hamilton had removed his shoes and she realised just how considerate he really was. His big brothers would be proud of him.

'Must have been all that coffee Susie sent with us,' he agreed as he walked to the large refrigerator and opened it. In some ways it was eerie to walk around someone else's home but it was just the way country hospitality was. 'Hungry?'

'Not really. Perhaps a cup of tea.'

Hamilton nodded and closed the fridge, opening cupboards, finally locating herbal tea. As Ruby watched him pad silently around the strange kitchen in his socks, she felt the world at large start to disappear, leaving herself and Hamilton together in this confined atmosphere. She sat on a stool at the breakfast bar, put her elbows on the bench and propped her head in her hands, content to watch him.

'Ah, tea,' he said with triumph, his voice still soft as he took a few boxes down from the cupboard. When he turned to face her, he stopped, becoming aware she was watching him rather intently. He slowly made his way to the bench and put the teas down. 'We have chamomile...' His tone dropped as he held her gaze. 'Peppermint...' He leaned forward, breathing out slowly as he brought his face close to hers.

Ruby was only half listening to what he was saying. Instead, she watched as his mouth moved, forming words of some kind, whilst she wished his lips were pressed to hers. She swallowed, her heart hammering wildly against her chest. She'd been caught in this bubble with him several times before and right now she was determined that he wasn't going to put on the brakes yet again. She wasn't dating Geoffrey any more and right now she didn't really care whether or not he was going to leave Lewisville in the future. They were connected. There were no two ways about it and if he didn't hurry up and kiss her…

Bringing her face even closer, she parted her lips, their breaths mingling together. The house was quiet except for the sound of a ticking clock far off in the distance. There was no one else around. It was just the two of them, removed from Lewisville, removed from family, removed from rational thought. Him and her. Close. Intense. Desperate.

'Ruby. I'm trying to be strong,' he murmured. 'It's not working.' He gazed into her eyes, knowing he could lose himself in them for ever.

'This can't be wrong,' she whispered, her heart hammering wildly against her ribs, her head filled with nothing else but him.

'I've wanted to kiss you for so long.' He swallowed and and he knew for certain that this time there was no stopping what flowed so powerfully between them. He also knew if he kissed her, there was no going back. Things would change—for ever.

'Ruby?' Even if she changed her mind right now, he wasn't sure he could stop himself from following through on the one thing he'd wanted to do since seeing her again.

'Shut up and kiss me,' she instructed, and the next second her eyelids fluttered closed and she gasped as he closed the remaining millimetres between them and pressed his mouth firmly to hers.

CHAPTER TEN

THE heat, the tingles, the sensations that passed between them were like nothing she'd ever felt before. It wasn't that she'd had many boyfriends over the years but she was experienced enough to know there was something very different about the way Hamilton's mouth seemed to fit perfectly with her own.

Where she'd thought her heart had been hammering wildly before, it was now pounding out a rhythm so heavy she became light-headed. With infinite care he moved his mouth against hers, slow and sensual as though desperate to savour the moment. This was like nothing he'd dreamt, like nothing he'd imagined—it was far superior in every respect. Ruby tasted like forbidden fruits mixed with spring sunshine and her subtly scented perfume made an intoxicating addition to that.

He was determined to keep the kiss light, to

test the waters, to ensure this moment was one of pleasure. He had no real idea exactly what existed between Ruby and himself but the power that continued to build as she opened her mouth to deepen the kiss rocked him to the core.

Placing his hands gently at the back of her neck to ensure she didn't pull away, he shifted, their lips locked as he urged her to stand up, to move. She did, sliding off the stool, both of them shifting round the bench in symmetry. When she stood before him, he slid his hands down her shoulders to haul her close just as she slid her hands around his waist and up his back. Both of them sighed with pleasure at finally being able to give in to the attraction they'd been fighting for what seemed like for ever.

It was impossible now to hold back when both of them wanted so much more. Ruby opened her mouth, her tongue slipping out to tease his lips, to entice him, to drive him wild. His groan of desire mixed with appreciation made her realise just how much he wanted her. The knowledge gave her a thrill of feminine power. Desperate for more, she slid her hands lower and found the hem of his shirt and she slipped her hands beneath the material, coming into contact with his firm, warm skin, her body igniting with a wave of fire.

Hamilton broke his mouth free from hers, gasping in delight. It was only for a moment, and they both looked at one another intently before giving in to their feelings once more. Ruby grazed her fingernails lightly up and down his back and Hamilton thought he would melt into her as he shifted sideways, leaning against the bench and pulling her even closer to his body.

Her fingers against his skin were starting to tip him over the edge and he could hear warning bells from somewhere far off in the recesses of his mind. This was Ruby. She was like family. That may be so, his heart argued, but he'd *never* had a reaction like this, so intense, so immense, so…inconceivable.

Ruby's special, his mind rationalised once again, and it was that thought that helped him to find strength from somewhere and a moment later, as he gradually eased his mouth from hers, pressing small butterfly kisses to her cheeks, her ears and down her long smooth neck that he knew stopping was not only the right thing to do, it was essential.

'Hamilton,' she breathed as she rested her head to his chest, listening to the fierce pounding of his heart, pleased she wasn't the only one along for the ride.

'I think we may have unleashed a little bit more power than either of us expected,' he murmured near her ear, and Ruby smiled.

'You're not wrong.' She stayed where she was, content to be in his arms, to feel the warmth of his body so close to hers, his hands slowly sliding up and down her back, caressing her. It was almost five minutes later that she eased back to look into his deep blue eyes. 'What do we do now?'

Hamilton slowly shook his head from side to side. 'I don't know.'

'Oh.' She wasn't sure why she was disappointed. She wasn't sure what she'd expected him to say. Did he have regrets? Was he going to say it had all been a big mistake? Ruby's insecurities began to raise their ugly heads. Was he yet another person who meant so much to her who would eventually leave?

'I know I want to be able to repeat that kiss, to hold you like this, feel you safe and close in my arms.'

'Oh!' She sighed, pleased at his response. 'So do I…er, want to kiss you again, I mean.'

He smiled brightly at her words, dipping his head to brush a tantalising kiss across her lips. 'Why don't we take it one slow step at a time?'

Ruby nodded.

'This is a…big change—for both of us.'

She smiled up at him and pushed a lock of his hair back with her fingers. 'I want you to know, Hamilton, that I'm in this, too. Don't go thinking that you have to take full responsibility for what may or may not happen between us. We're going to explore this frighteningly natural attraction together. We'll sort it out.' We have to, she added silently, because if they didn't, if at the end of his contract in Lewisville he left and went to Tarparnii, leaving her behind, Ruby knew her heart would break. She'd thought, all those years ago as a silly adolescent girl, that he'd broken her heart and crushed all her dreams, but that pain was nothing compared to what could possibly happen in the future.

His reply was to press a gentle kiss to her lips. 'OK.' He angled his head towards the tea still sitting out on the kitchen bench. 'Still feel like a cuppa?'

Ruby shook her head and sighed, feeling the beginnings of a yawn starting to work its way to the surface. 'I think I'm ready to sleep now. You've released a lot of my pent-up energy and tension.'

'So glad I could be of service,' he remarked, before she slipped from his arms. He quickly put the teas back in the cupboard and together they crept down the hallway to the guest rooms, situated side by side. 'Goodnight, Ruby.'

'Yes.' She nodded. 'It *is* a good night.' With a smile she stood on tiptoe and pressed a kiss to his lips, sighing with delight that she was now allowed to do that. 'See you in the morning, Hamilton.'

He gave her hand one final squeeze before letting her go and heading into his own room. He sat on the bed, head in his hands, still concerned for what might happen next. The fact that the kiss they'd shared had been the best kiss of his life wasn't in dispute. With that kiss came a whole barrel-load full of questions. He liked being around Ruby. He liked spending time with her, joking with her, singing with her, laughing with her. They were compatible. But *they*, as a couple, were incompatible, especially with the lifestyle he wanted to live.

Besides, even if he chose to stay in Lewisville, what was he supposed to do? Brandon would return in July and Hamilton would be out of a job. It was clear the township and surrounding districts needed two doctors to service it but not three. It wasn't as though he didn't like living in a small community, because he was used to the ways of small towns, but there was so much more of the world for him to explore, to seek out, to experience. When his time was up in Lewisville, he'd be gone and Ruby would still be there… unless he could convince her to go with him. Would she leave? Could she leave Brandon and Vi? Would she come with him? Seek new adventures with him?

He leaned back on the bed and put his hands behind his head, staring at the ceiling. The idea of taking Ruby to Tarparnii, of introducing her to his friends, of showing her a different way of life, of travelling with her, the two of them together, probably should have filled him with dread but instead it filled him with an incredible sense of calm. He hadn't been looking to settle down, to enter into a long-term relationship, but the thought of Ruby with someone else tightened his gut into knots and made his head feel like it was about to explode.

The picture he *could* see was the two of them together. It felt right…but would she do it? Would she leave Lewisville…for him?

The next morning, Ruby couldn't help but feel a little shy when she first saw Hamilton. She quickly showered and headed out to the kitchen to greet their hosts, chatting with Russ's partner, Andie, as a large country breakfast was cooked.

Ruby sipped her coffee and nibbled at a piece of fruit toast, her thoughts on the man who had come to mean so much to her in such a short time. How would he react? Did he have any regrets? Did he now wish he'd never kissed her? What would happen next? Would he still leave Lewisville when Brandon returned? Even the thought of him gone caused her pain and she closed her eyes, trying to relax.

Last night when she'd gone to bed, separated from him by only a thin wall, Ruby had thought she'd have difficulty getting to sleep, but as soon as she'd closed her eyes, she'd drifted into a deep slumber, waking with the flavour of Hamilton's kisses still on her lips. The memory of his scent, of earthy, subtle spice, filled her senses once more and as she sat at the kitchen bench, cradling a cup of coffee, that same sense surrounded her again.

Ruby opened her eyes, her heart leaping into her throat at the sight of him standing before her, dressed in jeans and socks, light blue polo shirt, his hair still damp from his shower. She took a sip of her drink, wanting to appear unaffected by his presence, but then she swallowed the wrong way, immediately choking and coughing.

'You all right?' He quickly shifted around to pat her on the back. Was it her imagination or did his touch have a sensual feel to it? Did his words seem deeper, more intimate? When he rubbed her back, it definitely felt more like a caress and as she stopped coughing, giving him a watery smile, she was positive his warm hand lingered much longer than someone who was just trying to be helpful.

His body was close to hers, so much so that as she leaned back a little, it was almost like she was cradled in his arms. He made no move to shift away as he chatted easily with Andie. All the way through breakfast he seemed to stay as close to her as possible, smiling and engaging in conversations with others who came in for breakfast.

'Usually we have a lot more people here for breakfast,' Andie commented as they cleared the large kitchen table. 'But Russ was up early, taking some of the workers out with him to shift the stock to higher ground.'

Hamilton nodded. 'He mentioned something about that last night when we arrived.'

'Russ knows when the rains are coming—the bad rains, I mean. Floods, where one minute everything is fine and the next, the downpour is so fierce and unexpected it can make a trickling creek into a gushing, flooding river faster than a dingo after a rabbit.'

Hamilton's eyes were wide and he looked to Ruby for confirmation. She nodded. 'You've seen what it's like in Lewisville whenever it rains, how there's water gushing down the large gutters on the road.'

'Yes.'

'It's like that but...*more* so.'

'What about us?' he asked, and the words caused Ruby's heart to skip a beat until she realised that wasn't what he was talking about. 'Will we be safe? We still have a clinic at the Garner homestead tomorrow morning, don't we?'

Ruby looked at Andie, who shrugged. 'Russ is the one to ask but I can tell you it does take him a whole day, sometimes two, to move all the stock. It's a big job. That's why they all headed out earlier this morning.'

'We should be fine but we'll listen to the weather forecasts on the radio while we're here and take precautions,' Ruby offered. 'If we're stuck away for a few more days, it won't cause alarm. It's the way life is out here.' And right now the idea of being stuck with Hamilton, cut off from the rest of the world for a little bit longer, was actually quite pleasing. 'Besides, I have the satellite phone so can still get a message back to Vi to let her know our whereabouts.'

After they'd helped to clean up, Andie shooed

them away, telling them to go and get set up before the hordes started to arrive. Hamilton and Ruby did just that.

'Are you all finished?' she asked as she came into the front lounge room, which Hamilton had turned into his makeshift clinic room.

'Almost,' he remarked, surveying the room, a slight frown marring his forehead. 'There's something missing, though. I can't quite put my finger on it.'

Ruby stood in the middle of the room and looked around but she couldn't see anything out of place. Hamilton's gaze settled on her, dressed in flat shoes, linen shorts and a pale pink top. She was breathtaking. He also delighted in the way she'd once more scooped her hair off her neck, providing a clear path for his lips to enjoy. He wondered if she had any idea just how stunning she was. If she didn't, he was more than happy not only to tell her but to show her as well.

'Aha!' He snapped his fingers. 'That's it.' He crossed to her side, slipping his hands around her waist. 'I haven't kissed you good morning.'

At his words, Ruby smiled and sighed against him, resting her hands on his upper arms. He looked down into her face, wonderment and awe clearly visible as his gaze flicked between her eyes and her mouth.

'How remiss of you, Dr Goldmark,' she murmured.

'A fact I intend to rectify this very moment, Dr Valentine,' he returned, before lowering his head to capture her lips.

Once more Ruby was assailed with a multitude of emotions ranging from happiness to trepidation, from excitement to concern, from love to loss. She pushed the negative emotions away and focused on the here and now, of the feel of his mouth on hers, of realising that last night's heightened state of perfection had not been some weird fluke. His mouth moved tenderly over hers, unhurried and unwilling to escalate to where they'd found themselves last night.

'Good morning, my ravishing Ruby,' he whispered against her lips, before tilting his head to nuzzle her neck. Ruby sighed and wrapped her arms about him, loving the fact that he still seemed interested in her.

Love? The thought made her start to tremble and she eased quickly out of Hamilton's hold, turning away from him. Was it possible? She'd been so intent on fighting the attraction, she hadn't even considered it might lead to *love*.

At the sound of the homestead's front door opening, Ruby realised she had no time now to ponder such thoughts. 'Ruby?' Hamilton frowned a little, concern trickling through him. Why had she pulled away so quickly? Had he done something wrong? 'Everything all right?' he queried, dropping his hands back to his side. Was she having regrets?

'Patients,' she said, as a mother with four children walked into the lounge room, forcing Hamilton to put the multitude of questions plaguing his thoughts to the back of his mind. He'd have to deal with them later.

As it turned out, the clinic was a quiet one as many of the other property owners in the vast district were also out moving their stock in preparation for the coming rain.

'Even my two teenage boys are at home, bagging sand in case the creek running through our property floods,' one patient told him. 'You don't realise just how quickly those waters can rise.'

'So I've been told,' Hamilton responded, as he

finished writing up her case notes. By one o'clock they were done with no more patients to see. Ruby called through to the Garner homestead and cancelled the following day's clinic.

'It's not worth it,' she told Hamilton as they shared a cool drink on the front veranda. 'There'll be even more farmers wanting to focus on the weather rather than their health. And while it would have been fine to spend a few more days at one of the homesteads, getting back to reality in Lewisville is probably the best option to follow.' Even though getting back to reality meant she'd have to face the truth of what had transpired between the two of them. Here, sitting on the veranda, sipping a cool drink, smiling at him, knowing she could hold his hand or reach over and brush a kiss to his lips was liberating. It was like a fantasy world, where the rules and regulations of the real world had no say in what she did or how she felt. Logic, however, had to prevail. 'The last thing we want is to be stuck out on the road in the middle of nowhere because they're closed due to flooding.'

'Is the town at risk?'

She shook her head. 'Not badly. There's a reason why we have those deep, wide gutters in the main street,' she said with a small smile. 'We may get an ankle-deep river flowing down Main Street but that's about the worst of it. The last flood to hit the town was over a century ago.'

'What happened?'

'The town got wiped out, so they rebuilt on higher ground. We're all prepared for bush fires and floods.'

'You seem so nonchalant about it.'

Ruby shrugged. 'It's part of Outback life. You're nonchalant about snow and snow ploughs and tyre chains and black ice. You understand the dangers and you know how to circumvent them.'

'I guess. I'd never thought of it that way before.' He finished his drink and looked at her. 'So do we pack up and leave now? How do you want to play it, boss?'

Ruby grinned at him and he was pleased to see the smile return to her beautiful face. 'Boss, eh? I like it when you call me that. It'll take us about seven hours to get back to Lewisville so we won't make it tonight but we can certainly drive for a few hours and sleep in the car.'

He raised his eyebrows. 'Camping in the car?

Cool adventure.' He leaned over and pressed a surprised kiss to her lips. 'You got it, *boss.*'

Four hours later, Hamilton was driving down the long strip of bitumen that seemed to reach for ever in front of him. Ruby had decided to delay their departure so they weren't driving during the hottest part of the day. Instead, they'd taken their time packing up and helping out Andie with emergency procedures.

'If we're evacuated, I like to be prepared.' Andie pointed to two tightly packed bags. 'I have disks with all our photographs because people underestimate the importance of memorabilia when they're being evacuated. You can always buy clothes and food and furniture and everything else but you can never get back the memories of the past. Photographs are exceedingly important.'

Hamilton nodded in agreement. 'Especially if they're photos of loved ones who have passed away. I cherish the photographs we have of my parents.'

Ruby had listened to the wistfulness in his words and while both of their parents had died, they'd been left with vastly different emotions. In some respects they were really quite similar and yet in others they appeared to be polar opposites. Such as the fact that Hamilton seemed intent on travelling, on having adventures. Would he ever choose to settle down? Would he settle down with her? She had no clue what was going to happen now that they'd kissed, now that they'd broken through the barriers they'd previously erected. Now there seemed to be new obstacles in the way, new emotions, new questions she had no answers to.

He would definitely leave Lewisville in July and he'd definitely head overseas to Tarparnii. He was already contracted and she admired him for being reliable in that sense but what would happen when that contract was over? Would he return to Lewisville? Did he want to be with her? To continue to explore this frighteningly natural attraction that existed between them? What did she really mean to him?

She smiled as she watched him lift his index finger from the wheel as they passed another car, in the typical Outback greeting. 'You're really getting the hang of that,' she said. There usually wasn't much traffic on this road but, given the heightened state of affairs, people were wanting to get to where they needed to be sooner rather than later.

Hamilton grinned at her. 'I'm starting to feel like a real Outback bloke.'

Her smile widened, amazed at how infectious that grin of his could be. It was great to see him embracing this new experience but, then, Hamilton seemed to like new experiences, new adventures. In fact, she'd been quite surprised he saw sleeping in the car as a new adventure. To her it was simply something she did from time to time when it was necessary. She remembered him saying that some people saw a new adventure as anything that took them out of their comfort zone. If that was the case, it had been far too many years since she'd had any sort of adventure, as taking a step outside her own comfort zone was something she'd resisted.

Sometimes she wanted desperately to mix things up, to take time off, to say no to being on a committee, especially when it was taken for granted that she'd be there. She wished she didn't care so much what people might say about her if she did just take off the way Brandon had. They were a small community, everyone knew everything about each other's lives. While they all cared about each other, they also gossiped just as much, and she was always concerned that if she followed through on those whims and headed overseas, as Hamilton kept suggesting, what would the townsfolk say about her? Would they say she was ungrateful for everything they'd done for her? Even the thought swamped her with guilt.

She sighed and shook her head, clearing her thoughts, and watched as Hamilton raised his index finger as they passed another car.

'So what's it like, driving in Tarparnii? Do they have any little waves or signals?'

'As a matter of fact, they do,' he replied with a small nod. 'Their roads are half the size of this one, with either jungle or sheer cliffs on the side of the road. When a car, usually laden with ten to fifteen more passengers than it's licensed to carry, comes in the other direction, well, I'm not ashamed to say my usual signal was this—'

Hamilton lifted both hands off the steering-wheel and blocked his face. He quickly returned his hands to their former position. 'And it would be accompanied with cries of, "Please don't hit me!"' He laughed and shook his head, Ruby joining in with his laughter. 'Such a babyish reaction, I know, but I can't help it. It's freaky, driving over there.'

'Sounds like a real adventure.'

Was there a wistfulness in her tone? Hamilton looked from the straight, flat road to Ruby and back to the road again. 'It is.' He took a slow and steady breath before asking carefully, 'Have you been thinking of having some adventures of your own?' He waited for a minute but she didn't answer, so he continued. 'I know you've told me you're not a big-city fan but there are plenty of other places that you would simply love.'

'I love Lewisville.' He could hear the stubbornness in her words.

'And I love my home town of Ood but that doesn't mean I want to spend every second of my life there.'

Ruby shrugged. 'Why are you so intent on getting me to leave Lewisville?'

'I'm not trying to get you to leave, Ruby, I'm

trying to get you to see there's more to life than this obligation you seem intent on fulfilling.'

'Obligation? What are you talking about?'

'You're overly accommodating.'

Ruby bristled at his words, annoyed that he'd destroyed the moments of fun and happiness she'd been having with him. 'I am not. I'm a part of this community. I do as much as anyone else.'

'That's not what I mean.'

'Then what do you mean? Because you're not being clear at all.'

Hamilton breathed in, then slowly let it out. 'You feel that because the town so readily accepted a grieving fifteen-year-old Ruby, that they took you in and made you a part of their community—that you have to stay, living every second of your life there.'

'I *choose* to stay,' she said, but even she could hear the contradiction in her voice.

'What if you met someone…and he wanted to… marry you but he refused to stay permanently in Lewisville? What would you do? Would you go with him? Move?'

Ruby swallowed over the sudden dryness in her throat. Was Hamilton asking her to marry him?

Was he trying to suss out what might happen if he did? 'Is this a test?' she asked quietly.

'Yes, Ruby. It's a test. Are you going to let your misguided sense of obligation, your guilt, your fear stop you from having a life filled with intellectual stimulation? Happiness? Love?'

'I have those things in Lewisville,' she argued.

'Are you joking?' Hamilton shook his head. 'Of course you are loved by the people around you and, yes, you're probably happy, but nowhere near as happy as you should be. You are an amazing doctor, there's no doubt about that, but you could be so much more, and I'm not even talking about doing the odd GP refresher course. You're fantastic with young children, excellent with teenagers. You would make a wonderful paediatrician. You'd be able to bring guidance and hope to not only other communities here in the Outback but also other countries overseas. There are so many children in Tarparnii, with their big brown, soulful eyes looking at you while they cough and splutter, unable to understand why they're so sick. You have a sharp mind and the ability to do so much more, Ruby. It drives me half-insane to see you wasting all that talent, stagnating in Lewisville.'

Ruby couldn't believe he was talking to her like this. She shook her head, anger starting to boil deep inside at the way he was criticising her life. It didn't matter that one secret part of her, buried deep down inside, agreed with what he was saying, that she *could* leave to pursue further medical training, that she *could* hope to find a man who would love her for who she was, that she *could* achieve her dream of having a husband and family of her very own. She would do things so differently from how her parents had raised her. She would spend time with her children, she would be interested in what they were doing. She would do her best not to argue so much with her husband, to emulate the loving relationship she'd witnessed between Viola and Bill, but none of that was any of Hamilton's business.

'What do you know of what I *really* want, Hamilton? What right do you have to speak to me in such a way, diminishing and disregarding the life I've built for myself in Lewisville? You may want to head off on adventures, travelling and having fun, but you can't do that for ever.

When you've had enough, where will you go? Or do you plan to find yourself a wife, have a couple of kids and lug them around the world on your quest to find the next big adventure? That sort of life is the selfish life. That sort of life takes into consideration no one else's feelings except the one who is instigating the constant change. That sort of life provides no stability and no sense of permanence for children or the family at large.' Her green eyes flashed with intense anger as she glanced at him.

'And what I choose to do with *my* life is *my* business. Just because we shared a couple of kisses does not give you the right to apply your dictates to how I choose to live. If I want to stay in Lewisville for the rest of my life, that's *my* business, not yours.'

She pointed to a road siding up ahead. 'Pull in there,' she demanded. 'I need some air.'

Hamilton clenched his jaw at her words but did as she'd requested. As soon as he'd stopped the car, she opened the door and climbed out, slamming it closed behind her. He watched her walk away, her strides long and angry.

He'd wanted answers. He'd wanted to know

if what Ruby felt for him was something that could stand the test of time. He shook his head then thumped the steering-wheel in complete frustration. It was clear the intense moments, the mind-blowing kisses, the heart palpitations hadn't meant as much to her as they had to him. He'd be a complete fool to pursue her now, and yet… As he looked at her retreating back, her brown hair swishing angrily from side to side as she walked away from him, Hamilton knew his own warnings had come too late.

His feelings for Ruby were already too intense to forget and he knew she'd hurt him far worse than ever before.

'You're already in love with her, you idiot.'

CHAPTER ELEVEN

BEING attracted to Ruby was one thing but falling in love with her was something that had definitely not been on his agenda. He was fun-loving Hamilton. Finally free from the tight bonds he'd often rebelled against as a teenager. He hadn't planned on having a long-term relationship for at least another five years. He hadn't planned on feeling the way he did about Ruby. In short, he hadn't planned on losing his heart.

Three of his brothers had fallen in love and he and Bartholomew had chided them, teased them before swearing to remain bachelors. Now look at him. Once again falling in love with a woman who couldn't love him back. He realised now that what he'd felt with Diana had been nothing compared to how Ruby made him feel, but if she wasn't willing to meet him halfway, or at least even be willing to rationally discuss any sort of future they could possibly have together, he may as well continue to travel. Without her in his life… He shook his head, unable to even think that far ahead.

He glanced around the car, trying to figure out what they were supposed to do next. Were they going to continue driving or was it getting too close to dusk, when it would be dangerous to drive on the roads because kangaroos would be around? How much further could they drive before these torrential rains were due to hit? He shook his head. He had no real idea what was happening and the one person who could answer all his questions would probably never speak to him again.

'You've really stuffed it up this time, Ham,' he told himself, and shook his head. He opened the glove box, looking for a map to try and figure out where they were, and spotted the satellite phone. He picked it up and pressed a button, amazed when he received a dial tone. Before he really knew what he was doing, he'd tapped in a number and waited as the phone began to ring.

'Edward Goldmark,' came the answer at the other end.

'Bro.'

'Ham! How are things in Lewisville?'

'Terrible.'

'What? What's wrong? Is Viola OK? Ruby? What's—?'

'Everyone's fine. Healthy. Good.' Hamilton rubbed his eyes with his free hand.

'Then what's wrong?'

'It's me. I've…' Hamilton stopped and shook his head. 'I think I've fallen in love, bro, and I don't have a clue what to do.' For years Hamilton had been desperate for his brothers to see him as an equal, to stop treating him like the baby of the family, to let him make his own mistakes. Yet now he was desperate for some sort of advice and was therefore completely shocked when all he heard coming down the line was deep, male laughter.

'Hey, bro. Welcome to the club!'

'Edward, this isn't funny.'

'No. It's hilarious. The only other thing that would be funnier was if this call was from Bart!'

'Edward, what do I do?'

'It's Ruby, isn't it?' Edward nodded. 'She was always sweet on you. I remember all those years ago when I came to pick you up from Lewisville at the end of your holiday there. Oh, the way she'd looked at you—as though you were the best thing since sliced bread.'

'Yeah, well, now she looks at me as though I'm old, disgusting, mouldy bread.'

Edward laughed again. 'Ah, it happens to the best of us, Ham. Hang in there, bro. If it's love, if it's *real* love, things will sort themselves out.'

'That's it? You're not going to tell me what to do?' Hamilton dropped his hand into his lap and looked straight ahead at the flat, uninviting land-scape surrounding him. If ever he'd felt alone in the wilderness, this was it.

'Nope. You're on your own, mate, but I'd say you're off to a good start.'

'Really? How's that?'

'You've admitted to yourself that you're in love with her. That's half the battle over.'

'What's the other half of the battle?' he asked, as he saw Ruby coming out of the toilet block and heading back towards the car.

'Getting Ruby to admit it.'

'How do I do that?'

Edward merely laughed again. 'You're smart, Hamilton. You'll figure it out.'

Hamilton exhaled harshly and said goodbye to his brother, stowing the phone in the glove compartment by the time Ruby returned to the car. Without a word, she climbed in, buckled her seat belt and crossed her arms.

Hamilton received the message loud and clear and started the engine. He figured if he simply pulled back out onto the road and continued driving, she'd tell him if he was doing something wrong…and she'd probably do it with great delight.

Ruby heard a loud crack, louder than a stock whip and more powerful than an aeroplane overhead. She sat bolt upright in her seat and almost hit her head on the roof, momentarily disoriented by her surroundings. Bright light was filtering in through the front windscreen and she realised they'd slept for far longer than she'd intended.

'What was that?' she asked, immediately shaking Hamilton awake. He was lying in the reclined driver's seat with a blanket half on, half off his clothed body, his hair ruffled, his face relaxed. Her heart flip-flopped at the sight he made but she quickly shook her head, telling herself to focus on more important matters.

After driving for another hour, the sun had started to dip and they'd been in danger of hitting a kangaroo if they'd kept on driving. She'd directed him to pull into another road siding, those being the first words she'd spoken to him since the last time they'd stopped.

'We'll sleep now,' she'd told him, and had reclined her seat as far as it would go, then turned her back to him and closed her eyes.

Now, though, something had woken her. She shifted again, realising she had a blanket covering her. She couldn't remember getting one off the back seat before she'd fallen asleep, which meant Hamilton had been the one to cover her, ensuring she didn't get too cold once the sun had gone down. How thoughtful. As she looked at him again, for one split second her heart warmed and filled with love.

Love? Could it be true? Did she really love Hamilton? Was this for real?

'Wha—?' Hamilton stirred and exhaled slowly before opening his eyes and looking up at her, all tousled and sleepy and absolutely sexy. 'Morning, my ravishing Ruby,' he murmured, his tone deep and husky.

Ruby tried to harden her heart at his words, at the way he looked, at how she wanted nothing more than to lean forward and press her mouth to his. Instead, she took a deep breath and looked away from the enticing sight he made. She returned her seat to the upright position.

Another loud crash of kettle drums surrounded them and this time Hamilton jerked upright in his seat. Ruby glanced up at the sky through the front windscreen and shook her head.

'The storm's coming. We've slept too long.' She frowned at him.

'What? Why are you looking at me as though the thunder is my fault?'

'Because you distract me, Hamilton. You make me forget all the rules I've ever learned about living in the Outback. Get out. I'm driving.' With that, she opened the door and climbed from the car, taking a good look at the sky.

He quickly exited and came around to stand beside her. 'I know you don't want to talk to me but just for the moment, can you please explain what's happening?'

Ruby pointed to the big clouds rolling across the sky. 'That thunder is quite a distance away and yet it woke me up.'

'And that's bad?'

She glared at him again as though he had two heads. Hamilton shrugged and spread his arms wide. 'What? Where I come from, big black clouds like that mean snow. I'm learning.'

Ruby rolled her eyes. 'Those clouds mean storms and storms out here don't mean the rain comes down in enormous big drops, it means it comes down in enormous big buckets.'

'Right. Good. Consider me educated.' He turned to look at Ruby and rubbed his hands together. 'What do we do?'

'We get in the car and drive like we're being…' She stared at the clouds for another second before heading around to the drivers' seat. 'Well, like we're being chased by the storm.'

Hamilton had managed to climb into the car, adjusted the seat and buckled the seat belt before Ruby put the car into gear and zoomed away from the siding, pulling out onto the road and slamming her foot down flat on the accelerator.

'No speed limits out here?' he asked, quickly

grasping the side handle grip for extra support. Ruby didn't answer him, instead concentrating on getting them moving as soon as possible. Hamilton looked behind him at the clouds in the distance. 'How far in front do you think we are?'

Ruby glanced in the rearview mirror and shrugged. 'Twenty minutes, possibly thirty.'

He raised his eyebrows. 'Are we gonna be…' he pushed his arm out in front of him '…swept away?'

Ruby looked over and then shook her head. 'Once that rain hits us, we won't be able to see to drive. It will dump around eighty to one hundred millilitres of water in a matter of minutes.'

Hamilton whistled.

'We'll be fine. We just need to get to higher ground.' Ruby concentrated on the road as they zoomed along, Hamilton still holding on for dear life. The scenery was starting to change from being flat and barren to having trees dotted here and there. That obviously meant there was water somewhere near. As they continued, he noticed more and more trees, grouped together and leading downwards. That had to mean that topographically they were already quite high up as in the distance he could see the tops of the trees, their green leaves starting to sway with the approaching storm.

'Out here really is a different way of living,' he murmured.

'What the—?' Ruby slowed the vehicle as she squinted, peering straight ahead. 'Oh, you have *got* to be kidding me!' She was slowing the vehicle at a rapid rate, working down through the gears, and a moment later they swung into a large rest bay area with a sign that read Laicises Owns Creek. Beside the sign was a car. A normal-looking hire car. Around them were large gum trees.

'A creek?' Hamilton asked as Ruby snatched up the satellite phone and climbed from the vehicle. Hamilton quickly followed her as she peered into the sedan, surprised at the heat surrounding them even though a storm was approaching in the distance. 'Geoffrey, it's me. I'm at Laicises Owns. There's a car here. Booster seat in the back.' She tried the door. It was locked. 'There are two empty travelling mugs in the front. We're looking at a possible two adults and one child.' She paused and then looked at the clouds racing towards them. 'About twenty minutes.' She paused again. 'Yes, I understand that, Geoffrey, but there are three people, possibly more, in danger. I'm not leaving.'

Hamilton heard the stubbornness in her tone and saw that lift of her chin, the defiance flashing in her eyes. He allowed himself a small smile as he opened the back of the four-wheel-drive and checked to see what emergency supplies they had. As she continued to talk to Geoffrey, he spotted a large coiled rope and a pair of heavy-duty gloves. Best take them. Never knew what might happen.

'Hamilton and I are setting off to find them and hopefully we'll get everyone out in time, but if not...' She stopped and closed her eyes, rubbing the back of her neck with her free hand and releasing a stressful sigh. 'You take care, too,' she said, and disconnected the call. 'Right. Emergency services are on alert. If we can just...' She turned to face Hamilton and found him standing there with the coil of rope over his shoulder, a medical kit in his hands and a pair of heavy-duty gloves in his back pocket. He looked...dynamic but now was not the time to be ogling him.

'Ah...good.' She pulled out a folded tarpaulin

and closed the rear door of the car. 'Let's go.' As she led the way down to the creek, she couldn't help but be pleased Hamilton was ready, willing and able to help. Then again, she remembered he'd not only been raised in the Snowy Mountains, where there would often be emergencies, but also that he'd worked in Tarparnii.

'I guess you're used to emergency work like this,' she said as they trudged through the scrub.

'I guess.'

'Would you often go out on rescues in Tarparnii?'

'No. More often back in Ood. Tarparnii has the odd problem but mostly it's just clinics and stuff.'

'And stuff?'

'Getting to know the locals, becoming a part of their culture. There are more ways to provide medicine than with a pill or an injection.'

Ruby stopped so suddenly that he bumped into her, his free hand coming around her waist. 'You are so right,' she murmured. 'Listen.'

He did and then he heard it. A child's laughter.

'How can they be laughing at a time like this?' she said between clenched teeth, allowing herself a brief moment of drawing strength from

Hamilton's warm touch before setting off. 'Hello!' she called. 'Hello!'

'Hello?' came back the faint answer, and as they rounded a corner Ruby finally saw her. A young girl of about seven years old was playing in the cool water of the full creek. The land was plain but the creek had previously cut its way through the arid surroundings. Ordinarily, this was a beautiful place to come for a picnic, to paddle and unwind.

It had been quite a number of months since she'd been here and she noticed that further down the creek a tree had come down, forming another barrier for the water to swirl around as it passed. The little girl was situated inside a bay, the creek having cut its way around a knoll formed by large rocks and fallen trees.

'Where are your parents?' Ruby called as she continued her way towards the girl. The girl pointed and it was then Ruby saw two adults standing a little way off, one with an easel and paints, the other with a large camera. Hadn't they heard her calling? She turned back to the girl. 'Get out of the water. *Now!*'

'But Mummy said I could play,' she countered with a pout.

Ruby started to seethe. Every muscle in her body was tense and filled with anger. 'Stupid tourists. They have no idea,' she muttered quickly. Hamilton put a reassuring hand on her shoulder, his voice deep, calm and soothing.

'You get the girl. I'll deal with the parents.'

'They're not even watching her! What kind of parents are they?'

Hamilton gave her shoulder one last squeeze, feeling like she was more angry at these parents because they reminded her of her own. He put the rope and medical kit down next to where Ruby had left the tarp. Then the two of them headed off in different directions.

Hamilton kept calling loudly to the parents but received no response. Were they deaf? If so, couldn't they feel the change in the temperature? In the air? Although it was still hot, for the first time there were no flies around, the warm breeze fanning his face bringing with it a hint of impending doom as the storm continued to approach. 'Hey! Hello, there!' he yelled, drawing closer to the parents. There was still no answer and it was when Hamilton was a stone's throw away from them that he realised they both had headphones in.

Within a few steps he was next to them and tapped them both firmly on the shoulder. They spun around, jumping half out of their skins at seeing him there. Hamilton scowled as they pulled out their earphones.

'What do you think you're doing?' He pointed behind him at the dark and stormy sky, a pre-warning mist starting to fall over them. 'There's a storm approaching. A bad one. This whole area...' he spread his arm around where they were standing '...could be flooding in a matter of minutes.'

The look of complete and utter shock on the couple's faces would have been priceless if the situation hadn't been so dire. 'Get out of here,' Hamilton said, gesticulating wildly to the path that led back to the car park.

The woman started to quickly pack up her paints but Hamilton grabbed her arm. 'There's no time for that.'

'But my work. My paint—'

A loud, piercing scream split the air, followed

by an enormous splash. Hamilton immediately looked back in the direction where he'd left Ruby and the girl.

'Dragon!' the father exclaimed.

'What?' Hamilton was more perplexed but wasn't really waiting to find out as he quickly made his way back to where he and Ruby had separated.

'Our daughter, Dragon,' the mother said, still trying to pack up her things, her hands fumbling with her equipment. The father had his camera around his neck and was only a step or two behind Hamilton when the rains hit.

'Whoa!' Hamilton had thought the rain in Lewisville powerful when one minute it was dry and the next minute he was drenched through, the water coming down like someone had turned on a tap, but this…this wasn't getting drenched, this was a deluge. When Ruby had said the rain would come down in buckets, she hadn't been joking.

He wiped the water from his eyes, feeling as though he was standing in the middle of a waterfall. He looked back at the parents, the mother now realising the gravity of the situation and ditching her equipment to make a beeline for her daughter. Water was starting to puddle around his feet. 'Ruby!' he called.

'Hamilton!' she yelled back. He'd just come around the corner in time to see Ruby standing in the water up to her waist, holding the scared girl who was clinging to her for dear life. Ruby waded through the water, the rain pouring down on her. Hamilton rushed to the edge and waded in, holding out his hands for the girl.

As Ruby handed the child to him, there was a sound like roaring thunder to her right and as she turned to look, she missed her footing. She could feel herself starting to sink at the same time she felt the weight removed from her hands. Instantly, she put her arms out to steady herself, safe in the knowledge that Hamilton had the child. The water seemed to be rising at such a rapid pace that where she would have been able to retain her balance only minutes ago, now she found she couldn't and went under. She struggled to the surface, breaking it only to gasp in a breath as her other leg was swept from beneath her.

'Ruby!'

CHAPTER TWELVE

'RUBY!'

She could hear Hamilton calling her as her arms flailed beneath the surface. Desperation and fright pulsed through her as the water surged beneath her, tumbling her around. She tried to remain calm, to think clearly, to remember what she was supposed to do, but all logical thought seemed to have fled, with panic taking its place.

She was being dragged down, her clothes heavy, her lungs bursting, her arms trying to grab anything. *Reach out. Just reach out. Pull yourself up. Give me your hand. You can do it. You're a fighter.*

'Ruby!' Hamilton's voice seemed to be floating somewhere above her, muffled and distant. Was it any good? Fighting? The water pressed around her, squeezing her lungs until she thought she would burst. She closed her eyes, not wanting to know anything any more, and when she did, she was back, back in that mine shaft, a scared girl, buried alive. With a small pocket of air for breathing space, she'd opened her eyes to find she couldn't move her arms or legs. Panic had ripped through her and she'd tried to call out, but her lungs had felt dry and empty.

'Mummy?' she'd whispered. 'Daddy?'

Tears had rolled down her cheeks and she'd closed her eyes, feeling drained and heavy. Then as though from nowhere, she'd heard voices.

'Reach out.'

'Just reach out.'

'Pull yourself up.'

'Give me your hand.'

'You can do it. You're a fighter.' Those were the first words she could ever remember Viola saying to her, *You can do it. You're a fighter.*

Was she a fighter? She seemed to have made her way though many different obstacles through-out her life so far and now she was doomed to drown in the flood. Never to travel, never to get married, never to have children, and she wanted to do all those things with Hamilton by her side. She was certain of it. So why had she been saved all those years ago if this was the ending to her life?

'Ruby! Ruby!'

Hamilton's voice seemed to come from nowhere and Ruby tried to open her eyes, tried to see, tried to figure out where he was, but it was no use. There was too much grit and grime and her lungs were almost bursting with pain. Hamilton. Oh, Hamilton. She loved him so very much and yet she hadn't even told him. She'd been too scared to share that part of herself. Too scared to admit to him that he'd been right about everything, about the way she felt she owed her life to the town because they'd saved her. The way she'd thought it her duty to marry Geoffrey. The way she couldn't confess her love for Hamilton because one day he might tire of her and leave. Being alone frightened her so much. She was alone here. Alone right now. The water could have her, take her.

She tumbled over once more, opening her eyes to catch the briefest glimpse of Hamilton, leaning over her, reaching his strong, firm arms into the swirling water.

I love you.

The words were a silent prayer being sent from her heart to his and the next instant a band came around her chest, squeezing her lungs, and she forced herself to let go, to take a breath. She sucked in air, confusion and disorientation flooding her head. Rain was still falling, wetting her face, but, then, so was Hamilton as he kissed her cheeks and eyelids and forehead.

'Ruby. Oh, Ruby. I've got you. You're safe. I've got you. You're safe.' She was hauled close to his chest, her lungs still dragging in oxygen between the spluttering coughs. 'Ruby. *My* Ruby.'

'Hamilton?' She tried to say his name but found her throat hoarse as the rain kept pouring down on them.

'Shh. It's OK. Don't talk. I've got you. We just need to carefully make our way back to the bank.'

It was only then she became vaguely aware they were on a large fallen tree and that Hamilton had something firm and rough around his waist. The rope. He'd tied the rope around himself and secured the other end around the base truck of a large old gum tree. He had saved her.

Together, they shuffled and shifted their way to the end of the horizontal tree and once they were up higher on the bank, they collapsed, Hamilton ensuring she was lying on his chest, safe and secure in his arms. So tight and firm and steadfast were those arms of his that Ruby realised right then and there that he was *never* going to let her go. She wasn't sure how she could be one hundred per cent sure about that but she just was.

'OK. Enough rest time,' he stated, shifting a little to test the ground beneath them was firm enough to stand on and wouldn't be washed away with their weight.

'Kisses first,' she said, lowering her head so their lips could meet. She put everything she had into the kiss, letting him feel just how much she wanted him, needed him, loved him.

'Ruby, we—'

'Shh. I almost drowned just now.'

'I know. I was there. It was the longest thirty seconds of my life.'

'It felt a lot longer to me,' she confessed.

'My darling Ruby.' He kissed her once more but pointed to the track. 'We need to get out of here. I have a feeling the creek hasn't finished rising yet.'

'No.' She was still leaning against him, unsure she had the strength to stand, let alone walk. 'Uh—where's the family? Is the little girl—?'

'She's safe. You rescued her. They've gone back to their car. I told them to stay there until help arrives.' He shifted again and it was only then he remembered the other end of the rope was tied to a different tree, supplying him with an anchor throughout his desperate rescue. There was no way in the world he was going to let the woman of his dreams drown. He'd been searching for her all his life and now that he'd found her, he most definitely wasn't going to let her go.

'Sit still and catch your breath. I just need to untie myself.' He headed over to untie the rope and Ruby collapsed backwards to the ground, the rain pouring down on her, the roar of the creek—now a raging torrent—filling her ears. Yet all she could think about was Hamilton. He'd saved her. He'd literally and figuratively saved her life. How could she not have understood, not known that *he* was the man for her? *He* was the one she would spend the rest of her life with. Now, though, everything was crystal clear and as she watched him make his way carefully back to her, coiling the rope and slinging it over his shoulder, Ruby's heart filled with love. Honest to goodness, plain and simple—love.

'Come on.' He held out his hand as he reached her side and helped her to her feet. The instant she stood, though, her ankle gave way and she cried out in pain.

'Ruby? What is it? What's wrong? Is everything OK? Tell me. I want to help.' His words of concern tumbled from his mouth and she couldn't help but lean over and kiss him as his big strong arms came about her waist, holding her close.

'I've done something to my ankle. Probably just a twist.'

Before she'd finished speaking, Hamilton had dumped the rope and scooped her up into his arms. 'Then allow me to carry you to safety.'

Ruby linked her hands about his neck. 'It's too much. The ground may be too soft. It might not take our combined weight.'

'We'll go slowly,' he promised, and kissed her mouth, leaving Ruby with the feeling that he wasn't only talking about the walk back to the car but also their entire relationship.

* * *

'Just a sprain,' Hamilton said as he finished looking at the X-ray and handed her the films, knowing she'd want to see them. The love of his life was safely ensconced in a private room at Broken Hill Base Hospital. Little Dragon and her parents were down the hallway, being looked after by staff.

'You'll be fine in a week or two but you have to stay off it for the next few days.'

Ruby checked the film then lowered it, looking at him. 'But I can go home, right? I don't have to stay here, do I?'

'You need bed rest, Ruby. I know what a workaholic you are and I doubt you'll stay off the foot if you go directly back to Lewisville.'

Ruby reached out and grabbed his hand, desperation and concern in her tone. 'But I promise I won't. I'll be good. I'll do everything you say. Don't leave me.'

'Leave you?' Hamilton took her hand in his and sat down on the side of her bed. 'I'm never leaving you.'

'But I thought you were heading back to Lewisvi—'

'And leave you?' Hamilton shook his head. 'I'm

not leaving you, Ruby. Not ever.' He squeezed her hand gently and looked deeply into her eyes. 'I love you.'

Ruby felt her heart swell with joy. 'Are you sure, though?'

He laughed at her puzzled question. 'Yes. Why do you think it would be difficult for anyone to love you? You're bright and sweet and charming and caring and funny and gutsy and—' Ruby reached out and placed a finger on his lips but he only kissed it and continued. 'And I can go on and on all day about how incredible you are, my beautiful, wonderful Ruby.'

'My parents didn't think I was wonderful.'

'Yes, they did. Viola and Bill *loved* you with all their heart. So does Brandon and so do I— but in a completely different way from Brandon, you understand.'

Ruby smiled at his words, loving the fact that he could make her laugh at a time like this.

'You're special, Ruby Valentine. You're a woman of substance, of integrity, of valour, of—'

She laughed and this time put her whole hand over his mouth. 'All right. Enough already.'

Hamilton took her hand from his mouth and

turned it over to kiss it. 'I want to spend the rest of my life telling you how fantastic you are,' he stated. 'I'm sorry if that scares you because accepting it means taking a step into the unknown and I understand how difficult it is for you, but I'm simply not content to lose you.' He shook his head and gazed into her eyes, his throat thick with emotion. 'For one second today, I'd thought I wouldn't get to you in ti—'

'Oh, shut up,' she said, and urged his mouth towards hers, silencing him with a kiss. 'I don't want you to leave me,' she whispered. 'Not now. Not ever.'

'I won't.'

'And if I decide I can't leave Lewisville?'

'Then I'll stay, too. We can work it out. Together. I can work here at Broken Hill, commuting and helping out in Lewisville. Brandon could take more time off, do more courses if he wants to. I'm staying with you, Ruby.'

Her eyebrows hit her hairline. 'You'll sta—' She shook her head as she computed his words. 'But you…you've always been talking about your adventures, of getting away, of not being tied down, and—'

'That's because my life was meaningless, Ruby. Without you in it I had to fill it with travel and challenges.' He kissed her lips. 'But *with* you, my life is enriched. That's what I've been trying to get you to realise about your own life. You, me—both of us deserve a life that is enriched with love and happiness, and we can find that together. I love you, Ruby.'

'Oh, Hamilton.' She placed her hands on either side of his face and drew him closer, pressing a long and lingering kiss on his lips. 'I…I love you, too,' she said, stammering slightly over the words but knowing they wouldn't be difficult to say because her heart was hammering out such a wild tattoo with those exact words. 'I love you, I love you, I *love* you, Hamilton Goldmark.'

'Will you marry me, Ruby? Will you agree to be my wife, to be with me, to share with me, to laugh and cry and do everything with me?'

'Yes.' She laughed and tears of happiness and joy ran down her cheeks. He tenderly brushed them away and kissed her once more. 'Oh, Hamilton. You've made me so happy. I never knew it could feel like this and best of all you're giving me the one thing I've always wanted, so secretly deep down inside.'

'To be a true Goldmark?' he queried, and she looked at him with aghast surprise.

'How on earth did you know?'

His smile was slow and sexy, his eyes twinkling with delight. 'You'll have to torture it out of me!'

Ruby laughed and blushed and laughed some more. 'Hamilton!'

He kissed her and stopped only when there was a knock at the door. Viola rushed in but stopped short, seeing the two of them together, so close, so happy, so…made for each other.

'Vi.' Ruby held out a hand to her, eyes bright with tears of happiness. 'We have some news.'

A moment later, Viola's shriek of delight could be heard throughout the entire ward and soon there were quite a few more visitors to Ruby's room to find out what all the commotion was about. Finally, when they were alone, Hamilton eased onto the bed and slipped his arms around his fiancée.

'So…what's next?' he asked.

'You mean after we pick out a ring and tell all our friends and organise a wedding?'

He chuckled. 'Yes.'

'Well, you have made a commitment to Pacific Medical Aid to work in Tarparnii—'

'I'm not leaving without you, Ruby. PMA will just have to understand.'

'Of course they'll understand, especially as… I'm going to go with you.'

Hamilton looked at her. 'Are you sure? I don't want you to think I'm pressuring you.'

She shook her head. 'You're not. I feel the same way about you as you feel about me, Hamilton, and I don't care if we're in Lewisville, Tarparnii or even Timbuktu! I don't want to be far away from you.' She paused and nodded, as though pleased with this decision. 'It's time. It's time I flew the crazy coop. Time to start the next phase of my life…the time I get to share with you.'

Hamilton kissed her. 'And what a time we're going to have!'

EPILOGUE

'Is SHE ready yet?' Hamilton paced around Viola's front room, tugging on the collar of his shirt. 'These things are hot. Whoever said the guys had to wear suits to this Valentine's Day dance was an...' He paused, stopping his pacing, stopping his ranting as the woman of his dreams stood before him, dressed in a dark, sleek and incredibly sexy dress that highlighted all her curves.

Hamilton simply stared, one hundred per cent positive his tongue was hanging out on the floor.

'Well?' she asked, doing a little pirouette for him, swishing her hips and sliding her black-gloved hands down the tight-fitting dress. Her hair was up in a high bun with diamantés around it.

'Uh...' He tried, swallowing over his desire. 'I'm not sure you're going to make it to the dance,' he finally remarked, stepping forward and taking his fiancée in his arms. He moved from side to side, swaying her in a slow waltz.

'We have to go, Hamilton. I'm on the organising committee.'

'Everything will run fine without you. Besides, it's about time other people stepped up to the plate, taking over some of your committee commitments. I want to dance with you and you alone all night long. I'm a possessive man who is madly in love with his desirable...' he kissed her exposed neck on one side '...sexy...' he kissed the other side of her neck '...fiancée.' He pressed a firm kiss to her mouth. 'I will never tire of kissing you, my Ruby.'

'I'm pleased to hear it,' she returned, sliding her arms about his neck, not caring in the slightest if they didn't make it to the dance. He was right. It was time for her to pull back on her community duties, to allow others the chance to be givers. In July, she and Hamilton were both scheduled to head to Tarparnii with PMA and they'd be going as husband and wife.

Her life was really starting to happen and it was all because of him, the man who held her as though she were the most precious, most important, most beloved person on the face of the earth. *This* was what real love was all about and she couldn't believe how fortunate she was to have found it. Her heart was beating in time with his, the two of them forming one entity.

'Happy Valentine's day, my love,' Ruby whispered in his ear.

Hamilton's lips curved into that slow and sexy smile that set her heart racing with excitement. 'Even though you're soon going to be Mrs Ruby Goldmark, you will *always* be my Valentine.'

* * * * *

Mills & Boon® Large Print
Medical

March

HER MOTHERHOOD WISH	Anne Fraser
A BOND BETWEEN STRANGERS	Scarlet Wilson
ONCE A PLAYBOY...	Kate Hardy
CHALLENGING THE NURSE'S RULES	Janice Lynn
THE SHEIKH AND THE SURROGATE MUM	Meredith Webber
TAMED BY HER BROODING BOSS	Joanna Neil

April

A SOCIALITE'S CHRISTMAS WISH	Lucy Clark
REDEEMING DR RICCARDI	Leah Martyn
THE FAMILY WHO MADE HIM WHOLE	Jennifer Taylor
THE DOCTOR MEETS HER MATCH	Annie Claydon
THE DOCTOR'S LOST-AND-FOUND HEART	Dianne Drake
THE MAN WHO WOULDN'T MARRY	Tina Beckett

May

MAYBE THIS CHRISTMAS...?	Alison Roberts
A DOCTOR, A FLING & A WEDDING RING	Fiona McArthur
DR CHANDLER'S SLEEPING BEAUTY	Melanie Milburne
HER CHRISTMAS EVE DIAMOND	Scarlet Wilson
NEWBORN BABY FOR CHRISTMAS	Fiona Lowe
THE WAR HERO'S LOCKED-AWAY HEART	Louisa George

Mills & Boon® Large Print
Medical

June

FROM CHRISTMAS TO ETERNITY	Caroline Anderson
HER LITTLE SPANISH SECRET	Laura Iding
CHRISTMAS WITH DR DELICIOUS	Sue MacKay
ONE NIGHT THAT CHANGED EVERYTHING	Tina Beckett
CHRISTMAS WHERE SHE BELONGS	Meredith Webber
HIS BRIDE IN PARADISE	Joanna Neil

July

THE SURGEON'S DOORSTEP BABY	Marion Lennox
DARE SHE DREAM OF FOREVER?	Lucy Clark
CRAVING HER SOLDIER'S TOUCH	Wendy S. Marcus
SECRETS OF A SHY SOCIALITE	Wendy S. Marcus
BREAKING THE PLAYBOY'S RULES	Emily Forbes
HOT-SHOT DOC COMES TO TOWN	Susan Carlisle

August

THE BROODING DOC'S REDEMPTION	Kate Hardy
AN INESCAPABLE TEMPTATION	Scarlet Wilson
REVEALING THE REAL DR ROBINSON	Dianne Drake
THE REBEL AND MISS JONES	Annie Claydon
THE SON THAT CHANGED HIS LIFE	Jennifer Taylor
SWALLOWBROOK'S WEDDING OF THE YEAR	Abigail Gordon